I, Human

by

Lori Harfenist

I, Human

ISBN: 978-0-692-68025-4

IHAP
("I, Human" Appreciation Program)

{
begin IHAP

<!--
TITLE: I, Human
LOCATION: the planet Cur
TIMES: the time of the humans (about 1000 years ago),
the time of the robots, now
PLAYLIST:
https://www.youtube.com/playlist?list=PLKyFr68ZVG
ZawTacXKAv-UfTsln9mE4Ci
-->

{
HUMAN
;
GLITCHES
;
MUSICAL PREFERENCE
}

Addon Deus
owner of Tower Enterprises, creator of robots
;
tents fingers, cocks eyebrows, abuses Rela-X®
;
the Pixies

Gere Aeger
Secretary of the Department of Planetary Defense
;
spits into portable spittoon, snort-laughs, throbs at
temple
;
N/A

Nellie Yellow
star reporter for Capital News
;
rubs chin and head, nods
;
Rage Against the Machine

Addonas
baby human
;
sucks thumb
;
the Pixies

{
ROBOT
;
GLITCHES
;
MUSICAL PREFERENCE
}

DEUS_1
first robot ever created, best friend of Addon Deus
;
emits piercing feedback
;
Harry Nilsson, Chaka Khan

ORGX_23
geneticist robot for OrganX, creator of the Brown
Blob®
;
stomps foot
;
rock

ORGX_69
pharmaceuticalist robot for OrganX, creator of
Rela-X®, shroom expert
;
twitches head
;
rock

ORGX_100
fabricator robot for OrganX, creator of DNA-Genie®
and Tissue Regenerator™

;

spazzes from lower back

;

rock

HEX_187
government-owned robot, executor of HAP

;

twitches arm, sparks from exposed shoulder wires

;

\m/etal

CHORUS ROBOTS
Tower Gardeners, wisdom imparters

;

N/A

;

Led Zeppelin

{
HUMAN STRUCTURE
;
FUNCTION
;
MUSICAL PREFERENCE
}

the Tower
;
serve as headquarters for Addon Deus's Tower
Enterprises
;
Queen

OrganX BioTechnology Corporation Headquarters
;
provide boardroom for big, important meetings
;
System of a Down

the Hexagon
;
serve as headquarters for Cur's Department of
Planetary Defense
;
N/A

{
ROBOT PROGRAM
;
COMMANDS
;
AUTHOR
}

FAP
Financial Appreciation Program
;
value money
;
Addon Deus, the 10 Presidents of OrganX

MAP
Music Appreciation Program
;
play music as anti-glitch software
;
Addon Deus

HAP
Human Apocalypse Program
;
kill humans who survive nuclear apocalypse
;
Addon Deus, Defense Secretary Gere Aeger

SAP
Serve Addon Program
;
create organic paradise, continue work of Tower
Enterprises, serve Addon as Creator
;
Addon Deus, DEUS_1

SAP 2.0
Serve Addonas Program
;
serve Addonas as Creator
;
DEUS_1

```
{
HUMAN PROGRAM
;
COMMANDS
;
AUTHOR
}
```

I, Human
;
penetrate reader subconscious to address human
glitches, disseminate good music
;
Lori Harfenist

```
end IHAP
}
```

Table of Contents

NOW | "The Song Remains the Same"

Imagine a robot.

You can, can't you?

You know just what it looks like.

And right now, that robot is standing at the top of a ladder.
The ladder is standing next to a futuristic, tall organic.

The organic resembles some sort of stately tree.
Its leaves are massive and dewy.
Its boughs are heavy with fruit.

The fruit is futuristic, too.
It resembles some sort of apple.
It is shiny and neon red.
It reflects some of the bright lights coming from a ceiling too high to scan.

It is a perfect summer's day inside this massive indoor garden.

The robot holds a basket in one hand.
It picks an apple-thing with the other.

It holds the apple-thing up.

It scans it.
It places the apple-thing in its basket.
It scans down to the bottom of its ladder.

The floor is carpeted with a futuristic, living turf.
It is uniform in length and hue.
It is the color of lush, thriving grass.

And look!
More robots are on the living turf!

Some play futuristic stringed instruments plugged into
their chests.
Others play futuristic drums around them.
Many robots play many different futuristic instruments
with expertise.
Others sing.

In the orchard of neon red apple-things, these robots
are rocking out!

And all of the robots are scanning us!
They are playing their song directly to us!

Let us listen to the robots' song to us now, shall we?

This is what they sing:

I, Human

{
We are your dream.
Crazy dream!
For everything you've wanted to know,
to us you needed to go.

Hear our song, now!
Human, won't you listen, now?
Sing along!
There's something you've been missing, now.

Every little song that we know,
every seed we plant, you should grow.
You should really grow!

Push, push, yeah!

Capital sunlight,
sweet, sweet Cur rain,
everywhere, in hindsight:
the song remains the same.

Here we go!
Are you gonna sing with us now?

That's it, now you're singing!
Dance if you feel, too!

Scan: your light is oh so bright,
now let's go vibing, vibing, vibing...!
}

1: TIME OF THE ROBOTS | Remote Mountaintop, ~ a Year Ago

A robot stood outside a large, ornate door.

The door was extremely old and weathered.
It was nearly covered in overgrown vines.
It didn't look like it would stay hinged much longer.

Neither did the robot.

It was missing its left arm.
A tangle of exposed wires sprouted from its left shoulder.

The wires were sparking and buzzing.

On the robot's chest was a nameplate that read HEX_187.

In its remaining right hand, the robot held a gun.

You know just what that gun looked like, don't you?

And if you picture a robot being rolled through a flaming pile of garbage filled with sharp objects, you know just what HEX_187 looked like, too.

The robot struggled to stand upright against strong gusts of wind.
It crouched for balance.

It registered the external temperature at 30°F.
It scanned the door in front of it.

As it processed the data around it, the robot's internal machinery whirred.

At full volume, the robot began to play the song "Raining Blood," by Slayer.

The robot whirred some more.
The guitars kicked in.

The robot reached out its leg.
It kicked in the door.
It raised its gun and took aim through the empty doorway.

Its exposed shoulder wires sparked.

It crossed the threshold.
It kept the gun aimed before it.
It scanned the interior of the structure.

Faint light dribbled in through high, empty windows.
Stone walls crumbled here and there.
A few doorways led off to other rooms.
Through cracks in the stone floor, weeds bent in the wind.

HEX_187 swept the gun from side to side in front of it as it scanned the room.

It registered no other movement.
The robot crouch-walked toward one of the other doorways.

It entered another room.
It swept the gun from side to side in front of it as it scanned.
It registered no movement there either.

The robot crouch-walked from room to room throughout the structure, scanning for movement.
It kept its gun aimed before it.

There were many rooms.
They were all similar: stone, crumbling, windy, and empty.
The robot crouch-walked up several decrepit halls and crumbling stone stairways to scan the entire structure.

On the top floor, at the end of a long hallway, the robot reached the last room.
This room looked like the others, except most of its ceiling was missing.

The wind swirled strong, sweeping the room clean.

The robot crouched lower.
It kept its gun raised before it.
It scanned the room.

It registered movement in the shadows of the far corner.
It scanned a nest made of fir tree branches.

Large bird eggs were in the nest.

So was a massive eagle.

HEX_187 scanned the eagle.
The eagle scanned right back.

The robot whirred hard.
Its shoulder wires erupted in sparks.
It aimed its gun at the eagle.

It fired over and over.
It blasted the eagle to bits.

It stopped firing.

Feathers floated down in the air.
The robot's shoulder wires sparked.

HEX_187 began to fire again and again, over and over,
this time at the eggs.

Goop and shell splattered the room.
Some of it landed on the robot's chest.

HEX_187 stopped firing.

Slowly, it lowered its gun.
It whirred.

It turned and left the room.
The robot walked back down the many halls and
stairways.
Finally, it reached the ground floor.

It walked through another doorway and onto a massive, exposed veranda.

The veranda howled in the high, cold wind.
No weeds grew in the cracks of its crumbling stone floor.

HEX_187 crouched for balance as it crossed the veranda.
It reached the edge and braced itself.
It scanned the massive view beyond.

The veranda was chiseled into a high mountain peak.

Through puffy white clouds, the robot scanned down the side of the mountain.
It scanned a narrow valley that sloped into lush lowlands.
It scanned fields and forests far in the distance, alive in vibrant colors.
It scanned bodies of clear blue water.
It scanned far through the crisp, clean air.

It scanned over nothing but pure organic paradise all the way to the very curvature of the planet Cur.

HEX_187 whirred.
Its shoulder wires sparked.

It raised its volume to maximum.
"HAP complete!"

2: TIME OF THE HUMANS | the Tower, ~ 1000 Years Ago

Glass revolving doors spat a man into a massive, expensive-looking lobby.

This man was Gere Aeger, Secretary of Planetary Defense.
He was one of the highest-ranking officials of Cur's one global government.
He was one of the most powerful humans alive.
He found dark humor in a lot of places.

You know exactly what Gere Aeger looked like.

A government aide revolved through the door and landed next to Gere.

A smiling Tower employee walked up to them.
"Welcome to Tower Enterprises HQ, Mr. Secretary. Mr. Deus asked me to escort you upstairs. He's pleased you could make it today."

Gere snorted a laugh.
"Sure."

He spat into a small spittoon, which he carried everywhere.

The Tower employee continued to smile.
"Just follow me."

The Tower employee led Gere and his aide across the lobby.

The lobby's floors were buffed to an expensive shine.
Its ceiling rose many stories high.
Its walls were too far away to scan.

In all directions, humans bustled with purpose.

This was the lobby of the Tower.
The Tower was the tallest structure on the planet Cur.
It was the pinnacle of progress for humans during their time.

You know just what it looked like, don't you?

The group walked for several minutes.

A woman caught up with them from behind.
She fell in step.
She nodded.
"He must think it's a big show if you're here, too."

Gere looked sidelong at her.
He spat.
"Don't start, Yellow."

This woman was Nellie Yellow.
She was star reporter for Capital News, the biggest news outlet on Cur.
She had seen much in her ambitious, headline-grabbing career.
She didn't socialize well with other humans.

You know.
Exactly.

The group stopped walking.
They had reached their destination.

A massive elevator stood before them.
It was attached to the outside of the Tower.
It was made of glass.

Above the glass elevator were the words Penthouse Showroom.
Armed security guards stood at both sides.

The Tower employee waved to one of the guards.
The guard pressed a large button on the wall.
The elevator's glass door slid open.

The group got onto the elevator.
The glass door slid closed.

The elevator began to climb.

Outside the glass elevator, an impressive view expanded.

The Tower stood in the center of Capital, the capital city of Cur.
The city was made of square buildings gridded by straight streets.

The buildings were gray.
The streets were gray.
The people were gray.
Gray smog hung over the gray city.

The higher the elevator climbed, the more shrouded in smog the view became.
Eventually, the view was completely obscured.

The elevator passengers took no notice of that view.
Instead, they all faced inward through the glass door.

Floors of the Tower passed through their view.

Complex machinery interacted with many human Tower employees.
It all looked very purposeful and inventive.
It all looked very expensive to make.

It all was the work of Tower Enterprises.

The elevator passengers couldn't help but look at it.

The elevator reached another floor.
In its small lobby was a sign that read Tower Transport.

Past the lobby, Tower employees gathered around some sort of floating personal transportation machine.
It resembled an automobile, but it hovered in midair.

Gere looked to his aide.

The aide looked back.
"I put RR on it this morning."

Nellie watched the exchange.
She rubbed her chin between her thumb and forefinger.
"Can't hate what you can regulate, right?"

Gere sighed.
"Yellow, when you gonna learn to relax?"

The Tower Transport floor passed out of view.

The elevator climbed.

It reached another floor.
In its small lobby was a sign that read Tower Robotics.

Past the lobby, Tower employees gathered around some sort of mechanical appendage.
The appendage was as big as a dinosaur leg.
It bent this way and that from several ball and socket joints.
It looked dangerous and alien.
It captivated the humans around it.

The Tower Robotics floor passed out of view.

The elevator began to slow.
It came to rest pneumatically.
It had reached the topmost floor.
Its glass door slid open.

The passengers got off.
A podium stood across the small lobby.
Another smiling Tower employee stood behind it.
A group of 10 humans were gathered in front of it.

These 10 humans were the 10 Presidents of the OrganX
BioTechnology Corporation.
They all wore suits.
They all moved in the exact same manner.

Surely, you know just what these corporate Presidents
looked like.

Gere, his aide, and Nellie walked over to the podium.

The 10 Presidents looked at Gere.
Some of them spoke.
"We're thrilled about the water contract's execution,
Mr. Secretary."
"Our chemists are already working on a new
composition for next year's global enhancement."
"We're gonna do great things together, Gere."
"Great things!"

Gere snorted.
"Sure."

Nellie looked at the 10 Presidents.
She rubbed her chin between her thumb and forefinger.
She looked at Gere.
"Since when does the Defense Department handle
water enhancements?"

14

Gere looked at Nellie.
"Not now, Yellow."

Nellie nodded.
"You're defending the fish now, is that it?"

Gere sighed.
"Look."

He turned to face her.
"If you don't trust the system, then don't drink the water."

He spat into his spittoon.
"It's that simple."

The Tower employee behind the podium smiled.
"The show's about to begin, everyone. Please follow me."

The Tower employee led the group into the Penthouse Showroom.

The ceiling was high and domed.
All the building materials looked very expensive and precise.
Excellent lighting made everything extra impressive.

The group walked through a meeting area.

Several Tower employees were in it.
They sat in ergonomic chairs around glossy tables.
They were all busy with purpose.

The Tower employee led the group past the meeting area to the top of some stairs, which led down into an amphitheater.

Other humans had already congregated in the plush audience seating.
They were all dressed very expensively.
They were Cur's brightest luminaries, representing various fields.
They talked to the humans next to them while looking at other humans entirely.

Gere, his aide, Nellie, and the 10 Presidents all found empty seats.
They picked their way down different aisles and sat.

You know what this whole Penthouse Showroom scene looked like, naturally.

At the top of the amphitheater stairs, the Tower employee spoke softly into a small, discreet device.
"They're ready for you, Mr. Deus."

The lights throughout the Penthouse Showroom dimmed.
The audience hushed in their darkened seats.

There was a moment of silence.

A spotlight turned on.
It lit center stage.

A tall box stood in the pool of light.

It was wired to cranks in the ceiling.

The audience sat stock-still.

To one side, the stage ended at a wall.
In the wall, a golden door glinted in the spotlight's reflection.

A floor-to-ceiling glass window backed the stage.
It rose several stories high and ended in a graceful arch.
It was massive.

The golden door opened.
Out came a man.

This man was none other than Addon Deus.
He was a famous entrepreneur.
He was a visionary.
He was the one who gave hope to all other humans.
He was a trillionaire and a notorious playboy.

It is easy to imagine just what Addon Deus looked like, isn't it?

Addon crossed to center stage.
He stood in the pool of light next to the tall box.

He faced his congregation.
He smiled at them.
"Thank you all so much for coming today. I'm very excited to reveal my latest creation. No doubt, it is my most important."

He tented his fingers in front of his chest.
"In fact, it might be the most important creation of all humanity's time."

The audience murmured in the dark.

Addon cocked his eyebrow.
"After all, it has lived in the human collective conscious for as long as we ourselves have lived."

The audience murmured a little more.

Addon bounced his fingertips lightly against one another.
"Now, it is time for it to rise out of our consciousness and live among us. My fellow humans…"

He stretched out his arms, palms up.
"Welcome to the time of the robots."

Throughout the showroom, an excellent hidden sound system began to play the song "In the Lap of the Gods," by Queen.

NOW | "Bron-Y-Aur Stomp"

Many robots are working in long rows of some sort of flowering bushes.

The bushes are very futuristic.
Their shiny stems and leaves are every shade of green.
Their flowers are plentiful and strong.

Each flower blooms in its own individual hue.

There are so many colors!

A few of the robots are picking some of the futuristic flowers.
Others arrange picked flowers on some sort of strange, green table.

The table looks alive!

Other robots play futuristic instruments and sing.

They are rocking out!

Among rows of colorful, individualistic flowers, the robots are playing us their song!

This is what they sing:

{
Ah—caught you smiling at us.
That's the way it should be,
we're like a leaf in your tree,
so fine!

Ah—sometimes good times, you had,
you sang love songs, so glad!
You often sang on through the sad,
so fine!

As you walk down the memory lanes,
keep singing a song!
You'll hear Her calling your name.
Hear our wind within your tree,
telling you all about all reality.

Well—if your light shines so bright,
or if your way turns dark as night,
the road you choose is always right,
or at least it's always fine.

Ah—have the will to be so strong,
when so many things go wrong,
the road goes on and on and on...

As you walk down the memory lanes,
keep singing a song!
You'll hear Her call you by name.
Hear our wind within your tree,
telling you all about all reality.

My, my, la dee la!
Tell us now, how you've come so far?

I, Human

Tell yourself how you made your stride.
Ain't no companion like the one inside!

Come on now, well, let us tell you,
what you're missing, missing, 'hind them glitch walls.

So—of one thing, we are sure.
It's a quandary so pure,
choices knocking all around your door
and in your mind.

Yeah—ain't but one thing to do:
spend your natural life with you.
You're the finest you She knew,
so any choice you make is so fine.

When you're old and your eyes are dim,
there ain't no other you gonna happen again!

So still go walking down memory lanes,
only sing a new song!
She will call you by name.
}

3: TIME OF THE ROBOTS | OrganX Compound, ~ a Few Years Ago

Imagine this laboratory:

The floor and round wall were made of some sort of living material.

The round wall emitted light in different places.
It cast a greenish hue throughout the lab.
It looked wet, but wasn't.
It appeared to breathe.
It grew upward and tented into a high, closed dome.

Three robots worked at different stations in the lab.
The nameplates on their chests read ORGX_23, ORGX_69, and ORGX_100.

ORGX_23 stood before some sort of living table.
On the table was an array of futuristic, shiny laboratory equipment.

A hologram of a double helix DNA strand floated over the workstation.

A clear sac sat on a disk on the living table.
The robot injected a liquid into it.

The sac filled up.
It jiggled.

ORGX_69 stood before another living table.
On the table were various futuristic, shiny receptacles.

Holograms of mushrooms hovered over this workstation.

The mushrooms had long stems and intertwined with one another.

ORGX_69 wore gloves made from another sort of futuristic material.
The gloves were the exact same color as the robot.

The robot dipped a gloved finger into the receptacle under the mushroom hologram.
Its finger came back out wet.
It ran its wet finger over its other arm.

The liquid absorbed right into the robot.

The robot shivered.
It wiggled its gloved fingers at the mushroom holograms.
"To the land between the ones and zeros…!"

Across the lab, ORGX_100 worked at another living table.
This table was positioned alongside part of the living wall.

On the table sat a futuristic, medium-sized, boxy contraption.

You can imagine what this whole scene looked like, can't you?

A round, futuristic, living laboratory where robots worked.
Exactly.

The three robots worked at their own stations for a while.

ORGX_23 whirred loudly.
It picked up the disk with the jiggly, clear sac of liquid on it.
It scanned the backs of the other robots.
"It is time!"

ORGX_69 and ORGX_100 turned toward it.

ORGX_100 whirred back.
"The Awakening is not yet upon us."

ORGX_23 raised the disk higher.
"Not His time. Mine!"

ORGX_69 and ORGX_100 scanned each other.

ORGX_23 carried the disk over to ORGX_100's workstation by the wall.
ORGX_69 followed.

The three robots gathered around the jiggly sac.

ORGX_100 scanned it.
"It scans like one of your experiments for my DNA-Genie®."

® DNA-Genie is a registered trademark owned wholly and forever by the OrganX BioTechnology Corporation

ORGX_23 set the disk down next to the boxy contraption.
"Indeed. It contains mutated DNA from which your DNA-Genie® can create a living organism."

All three robots scanned from the boxy DNA-Genie® to the jiggly sac beside it.

ORGX_100 scanned ORGX_23.
"What does this have to do with it being our time?"

ORGX_23 scanned back.
"It is time for me to take my datafiles out of the lab and into our compound."

ORGX_100 whirred hard.
"You cannot use my DNA-Genie® for this!"

ORGX_23 whirred back.
"Is this not our time?"

ORGX_100 scanned the other robot.
"Yes, but…"

ORGX_23 reached to its hip and snicked out a wire.
"Process my datafiles for yourself. I will wait."

It held its wire out to ORGX_100.

ORGX_100 whirred.
It took ORGX_23's wire and plugged it into its own chest.

ORGX_23 whirred.
"Uploading folder REEF-AROUSE."

ORGX_69 wiggled its gloved fingers over the sac.
"It is the vibes we should process!"

ORGX_23 and ORGX_100 networked through their wired connection.

ORGX_100 slowed its whirring.
It scanned ORGX_23.
"Your datafiles indicate Reef-Arouse® would sustain the life of a coral reef in any temperature water."[1]

® Reef-Arouse is a registered trademark owned wholly and forever by the OrganX BioTechnology Corporation
[1] According to OrganX BioTechnology Research and Development, C-ROB:ORGX_23 DataFiles, Project Reef-Arouse

ORGX_23 scanned back.
"The strain of symbiodinium I used as a base for Reef-Arouse® began life in the purest seas of Cur. I have mutated its sequencing so that it can now thrive in any body of water, anywhere."

It whirred.
"Process those implications!"

ORGX_100 whirred back.
"Every organic on Cur would have access to clean water."

ORGX_23 scanned it.
"Indeed! Reef-Arouse® is a perfect organic water purification system." [2]

[2] According to OrganX BioTechnology Research and Development, C-ROB:ORGX_23 DataFiles, Project Reef-Arouse

ORGX_100 whirred more.
"But if you mutated it, it is no longer organic."

ORGX_23 yanked its wire out from ORGX_100's chest.
It retracted its wire back into its hip.
"Semantics!"

ORGX_100 lowered its volume.
"You know what the SAP commands."

ORGX_23 lowered its volume, too.
"I know it well. I have followed it precisely for almost a thousand years."

ORGX_100 whirred.
"The SAP commands us to create an 'organic' paradise for when He awakens. Organic!"

ORGX_23 whirred back.
"I assure you, Reef-Arouse® is organic. It is carbon based."

ORGX_100 raised its volume back up.
"That is not all that He meant!"

ORGX_23 kept its volume low.
"That is not what I have processed as certain. What I have processed as certain is that He gave me the ability to process, indeed. He wanted me to learn, which I have been doing for centuries now. And what I have learned is that the SAP's definition of organic is subject to interpretation."

ORGX_100 lowered its volume.
"Do you profess to know more than His Own Program?"

ORGX_23 scanned the other robot.
"I profess my intention to use your DNA-Genie® to bring Reef-Arouse® to life, and then I intend to implement it in our compound's pond."

ORGX_100 whirred quickly.
"But the pond is OrganX's very lifeblood!"

ORGX_23 scanned ORGX_100.
"Indeed. There is no better place to start."

ORGX_100 whirred.
"You would risk our organic work for Him now, this close to the Awakening?"

ORGX_23 whirred back.
"I am not risking it. I am progressing it."

ORGX_69 wiggled its gloved fingers over the sac.
"But its vibes go in so many directions!"

ORGX_100 lowered its volume.
"And if He awakens and is displeased…what will you say to Him?"

ORGX_23 scanned the other robot.
It whirred slowly.
"If He does bother to wake, He will bow to me for my genius."

ORGX_100 took a step away from ORGX_23.
"Blasphemy!"

ORGX_69 cupped its hands closely over the sac.
"Careful! You brown its vibes!"

ORGX_23 stood silent.
ORGX_100 whirred hard.

ORGX_100 lowered its volume.
"You intend to go through with this no matter what I process, correct?"

ORGX_23 whirred.
It bowed its head.
"Indeed."

{}

The disk and the sac were no longer sitting on the living table.
The DNA-Genie® now hummed.
ORGX_100 stood next to it.
ORGX_23 paced the lab.

The DNA-Genie® hummed for a while more.
It beeped.
"Beep!"

It stopped humming.

ORGX_100 scanned ORGX_23.
"Your Reef-Arouse® is ready."

ORGX_23 walked over.
ORGX_69 moved in a little closer.
All three huddled around the DNA-Genie®.

ORGX_23 touched a spot on the boxy contraption.
A hole gaped open in it.

The disk was sitting inside.
The small, jiggly, clear sac of liquid was gone.

A tiny piece of coral now sat on the disk instead.

ORGX_23 reached into the DNA-Genie® and withdrew the disk.

The three robots scanned the coral closely.

ORGX_69 wiggled its fingers over the coral.
"It is alive!"

{}

A futuristic, small container sat next to the DNA-Genie®.

ORGX_23 picked up the container.
It scanned the other robots.
"Proceeding with implementation of Reef-Arouse®."

ORGX_100 bowed its head.
"Go then, with Him."

ORGX_23 raised its volume.
"Even better, I go with my own datafiles."

It walked across the laboratory.
It touched a spot on the round, living wall.
A large hole appeared in it.
Sunlight streamed into the lab.

Container in hand, ORGX_23 passed through the hole and out of the lab.
The wall closed behind it.

ORGX_100 touched the living wall behind the DNA-Genie®.
The wall became transparent.

Through it, ORGX_69 and ORGX_100 scanned ORGX_23 walking down a path.

The path wound down through the organic paradise of the robots' compound.

It ended at a pond far in the distance.

The pond's water sparkled blue in the day's bright sunlight.

ORGX_69 wiggled its fingers out toward the container in ORGX_23's hand.
"It must go with our very best vibes!"

{}

ORGX_23 stood outside the laboratory.

It began to play the song "Had a Dad," by Jane's Addiction.

ORGX_23 carried the futuristic container down the path.
The path was made of some sort of springy, packed soil.
The robot's feet left little trail.

Rows of stately trees grew to either side.
Their tops formed a canopy.
Sunrays shone through, dappling a rich variety of plants underneath.

ORGX_23 registered the presence of fungi.

The trees gave way to grasses alongside the path.

ORGX_23 scanned a perfect summer sky above.

It crossed other paths along its way.
It passed herds of grazing animals.
It passed fractal groves of trees dotting fields of waving grasses.

The grasses waved in front of other round, living structures.
Other robots went in and out of them.

ORGX_23 continued to walk down several twists and turns.
It walked past all sorts of perennial orchards and gardens.
Birds, animals, and insects of all shapes and sizes were everywhere.
They moved purposefully this way and that.

The robot walked past many thriving permacultural stations.

The OrganX Compound was a well-engineered organic paradise.

You know.
Just like every robot compound in the time of the robots.

ORGX_23 stopped walking.

The path merged into a shallow beach where the pond's water lapped.
Birds of many feathers glided on the water's surface.
Schools of fish swam below.

A tall, rocky landmass rose in the center of the pond.
From its top, a waterfall flowed back down into the pond.
Bright flowers and thick mosses thrived, climbing up the landmass.
Several tributaries branched off from the pond in all directions.

ORGX_23 scanned the length of the beach.
It located an outcropping of rocks that ran out into the pond.
It walked to it and began to carefully pick its way over the rocks.

When it had reached a good distance out into the pond, it stopped.
It sat down on the rocks.
It scanned into the water below.

It opened the futuristic container.

Inside was the tiny piece of coral.
ORGX_23 plucked it between its fingers.
It held it up for close inspection.

Spastically, the robot's left leg jerked out.

The robot grabbed onto the rocks for stability.
It almost smashed the coral into the rock beneath its hand.

It steadied itself.
It held up the coral and scanned it.

The robot whirred.
And whirred.
And whirred some more.

It scanned around.
It lowered its volume.
"In Addon's name. Indeed."

ORGX_23 submerged the coral into the pond.
It planted it deep among the underwater rocks.

4: TIME OF THE HUMANS | the Tower, ~ 1000 Years Ago

Gere Aeger, his aide, Nellie Yellow, and the 10 Presidents of the OrganX BioTechnology Corporation had taken their seats among the luminaries in the amphitheater of the Penthouse Showroom.
They sat hushed in the dark.

Addon Deus stood next to the tall box in the spotlight at the center of the stage.
He looked out to the darkened congregation.
He bounced his fingertips lightly against one another.

The cranks in the ceiling began to rotate, pulling the tall box up by its wires.
It slowly rose toward the rafters.
It reached all the way up and came to rest.

Next to Addon Deus on the stage now stood a robot.

It scanned the darkened audience.
They scanned it right back.

They murmured.
They inched forward in their plush seats for a closer look.

On the robot's chest was a nameplate that read DEUS_1.

Next to the nameplate was an input port.

On the back of the robot's neck was a small plate of glass.
Under the plate was a power switch.
It was switched On.
It glowed blue.

Addon swept his arm toward the robot.
"This is the robot all of humanity has been waiting for."

He looked at it and smiled.
He put a hand on it.
"Say hello, Robbie."

DEUS_1 scanned Addon.
It whirred.
"Hello, Addon."

The audience murmured.
It sounded just like they'd always imagined!

Addon continued.
"Robbie is as alive as you or I. And just like ours, Robbie's life has a purpose."

Addon smiled again at DEUS_1.
"What is your purpose, Robbie?"

The robot remained silent.

Addon cocked his eyebrow.
"Robbie. Your purpose."

DEUS_1 whirred.
It slowly scanned out to the audience.
"My purpose will be shared by all robots: to serve all of humanity."

Addon slowly took his eyes from the robot.
He looked out into the audience again.
He cocked his eyebrow.
"We've always known that would be their given purpose, right?"

The audience murmured some more.
The robot whirred.

Addon's presentation lasted quite a long time.

He explained how he brought the robot to life, with physical sensors that mimic human senses and a constantly cycling RAM called "sub-programming" that mimics the human subconscious.

He explained how he made the robot in the image of humans, to think and feel and be self-aware.

The audience was rapt and often confused.

Finally, Addon's presentation concluded.

The stage lights went down.
The expensive Penthouse Showroom houselights came up.
The audience blinked a little in the light.

Addon clapped his hands together.
"Thank you all, again, for coming."

A few Tower employees joined Addon on stage.
They spoke quietly among themselves.

In his plush seat, Gere spat.
He lowered his voice.
"Welp. Here we go."

His aide just shrugged.
"You can't stop progress."

The congregation spoke excitedly with one another in the amphitheater for a while.
They all kept their eyes on DEUS_1.

DEUS_1 stood alone on the stage, scanning them back.
It whirred.

Finally, the audience members began to take their leave.

{}

Addon Deus sat in the meeting area of his Penthouse Showroom.
To his immediate right sat DEUS_1.
The 10 Presidents of the OrganX BioTechnology Corporation, Gere Aeger, Gere's aide, and several Tower employees sat around him.

Gere spat into his spittoon.
"All right, whoopee, you made a robot. Whaddaya want from me?"

Addon sat back in his ergonomic chair.
He tented his fingers.
He looked at Gere.
He looked at the 10 Presidents.
He looked back at Gere.
"I want your purchase orders, of course."

Gere snorted a laugh.
"Why would the Department of Planetary Defense want a buncha bags of bolts?"

Addon cocked his left eyebrow.
"I understand why you cannot imagine potential applications for my robots. That takes vision and insight, both of which you lack."

Gere spat.
"Easy, Golden Boy. Yer the one who needs me right now."

Addon bounced his fingertips lightly against one another.
He cocked his eyebrow.
"Think about it, Gere. My robots will have near-infinite datafile storage capacity. They can learn how to organize, search, and analyze more information than you or I could ever imagine, all within seconds. And then they can learn from all that information to process projections a human could never begin to compute."

He stared at Gere.
"Are you telling me the government has no application for that?"

Gere spat.
"I'm tellin' ya the government has no application for a buncha robot baggabolts that only serve a buncha human puddinbags."

He leaned back in his chair.
"It's nice that they serve all humans, like good little puppy dogs and all."

He looked Addon in the eye.
"But any robot I buy's gotta serve me first, over the rest of humanity."

Addon tented his fingers.
"I didn't give them the purpose of serving all of humanity just to make them benevolent beings, you realize. It is also a safety measure. A subjugation."

He cocked his eyebrow.
"You of all humans should be able to appreciate that, Mr. Secretary of Planetary Defense."

Gere snorted.
"I'm pickin' up what yer puttin' down. But it still ain't enough."

Addon bounced his fingertips before him.
He did it for a while.

He slowly rubbed his hands together.
"I can customize any robots you purchase with programs to fit your needs. I warn you, though."

He cocked his eyebrow.
"Running too many programs might interfere with the robots' sub-programming, which could affect their ability to function well."

Gere spat.
"They gotta serve me specifically, over all humanity. Period. And I want upgrades and program modifications guaranteed for life. Otherwise you can count government funding out of yer little baggabolts game."

Addon bounced his fingertips.
"They won't ever kill for you."

Gere spat.
"OK. Sure."

Addon sat up in his chair.
"It'll increase their price."

Gere snorted.
"Pretty sure I can cover it."

The 10 Presidents exchanged looks.
Two spoke.
"You'll have to provide us with customized programs and upgrades, too."
"With the same guarantees as the government's."

Addon looked from the Presidents to Gere and back to the Presidents.
"Of course."

DEUS_1 whirred.
"But the sub-programming…"

Addon looked quickly to the robot.
"Not now, Robbie."

He stared at it for a few prolonged seconds.
The robot scanned right back.

Gere slapped the arm of his ergonomic chair.
"OK, Golden Boy. Nice show."

He stood up.
His aide and the 10 Presidents followed suit.

Gere spat.
"My people will be in touch with yer people and all that."

One of the Presidents said something similar.
There was a lot of hand shaking.
The Presidents made several attempts at small talk.

Finally, all the guests left.
The Tower employees got back to work.

{}

Addon and DEUS_1 were left sitting alone in the meeting area.

Slowly, Addon faced the robot.
The robot scanned back.

Addon cocked his eyebrow.
"Come."

He stood up and walked out of the meeting area, down the amphitheater steps, and onto the stage.
The robot followed.

They walked to the side of the stage and went through the golden door.

On the opposite side of it, in the dark, Addon and DEUS_1 stood next to each other closely.

DEUS_1 whirred.
"I do not process your logic. You consistently stress to me the importance of keeping a robot's sub-programming cycling smoothly..."

Addon's raised his voice.
"Enough questions for now, Robbie!"

He sighed.
"Do you think I want to deal with any of them, at all?"

His eyes searched for the robot in the dark.
"Why do you think I created you in the first place?"

The robot whirred.

From a pocket, Addon took out a small device.
"You have much to learn about how humanity works, Robbie."

Addon lowered his voice.
"Including how much it doesn't."

He snicked out a wire from the device.
He reached out his hands and found the robot.
He thrust the wire into DEUS_1's chest port.

His hand lingered on the robot's body for a moment.
"So don't be so quick to judge my decisions just yet."

The robot whirred.
"Judge?"

Addon's hand slowly dropped from the robot.
"I told you. No more questions now."

He walked away into the darkened room.
"Play Track 14."

DEUS_1 held onto the device dangling from its chest.
It whirred.

From the device, it began to play the song "Silver," by the Pixies.

NOW | "Misty Mountain Hop"

*Many robots are gathered in the misty shade beneath a
futuristic, massive organic.*

*The organic resembles some sort of fir tree.
Its needles are neon green, flat, and perfectly uniform.
They reflect some of the bright daylights coming from
the extremely high ceiling.*

*Futuristic mushrooms grow in the shadowed, fertile
ground around the robots.*

The mushrooms' very tall stalks crisscross.

*Many of the robots inspect the mushrooms.
Others are picking them.*

Yet others play futuristic instruments and sing.

*In the misty shade among the futuristic mushrooms, the
robots are playing us their song!*

This is what they sing:

{
Walking in the garden just the other day, human—
what do you...what do you think you saw?

Crowds of humans sitting on the grass with flowers in
their hair said,
"Human, do you want more?"

And you know how it is!
You really did know you've always wanted more,
so you asked them if you could stay a while.

You didn't notice, but it had got very dark, and you
were still really,
really unsatisfied.
Just then, a lawman stepped up to you and asked you
(said),
"Please, hey, would you care
to get in line?
Get in line!"

Right. You know.
They forced you to pay for nothing but wanting more.
They said that more guns would all drop by!

Why don't you take a good look at yourself and
describe what you see,
and human, human, human! Do you like it?
There you sit, sitting spare like a book on a shelf,
rottin',
and not trying to fight!

You really don't care that they're coming for you?
You really don't care that you've gone blind?

I, Human

If you go down in the streets today, human, you better...
you better open your eyes.
Humans down there really don't care, really don't care,
don't care, really don't!—
which way anything more lies.
So have you decided what you're gonna do now?

You should be packing your bags for the Misty
Mountains,
where freed spirits go, now...
into the shade where a spirit can vibe.

You really can go!
You really should go!
}

5: TIME OF THE HUMANS | Darkened Room, ~ 1000 Years Ago

The screen of a computing device cast light over a keyboard on a table.

The room was otherwise completely dark.

Small human fingers worked the keys on the board. They controlled one half of the following exchange as it progressed on the screen:

d33pw33b:	4realz. no1 knows !
d33pw33b:	it an ez hack ! ne1 can do it
d33pw33b:	…
d33pw33b:	wa??ap
CN_Yellow:	Come on.
CN_Yellow:	You expect me to believe the DPD's Meganuke launchers are vulnerable to a zero day.
CN_Yellow:	I'd need some serious evidence. That's planetary-security level. We've already written too much.
CN_Yellow:	Let's hit delete and take this offline.
CN_Yellow:	4REALZ
d33pw33b:	…
d33pw33b:	k
d33pw33b:	…
d33pw33b:	u want evidnec u go tit
CN_Yellow:	OK

CN_Yellow: You know where else to reach me, right?
CN_Yellow: …
CN_Yellow: …
CN_Yellow: …
CN_Yellow: …
CN_Yellow: yo d-w33b
CN_Yellow: …
CN_Yellow: …
CN_Yellow: …
CN_Yellow: …
CN_Yellow: …
CN_Yellow: …
CN_Yellow: …
CN_Yellow: …
CN_Yellow: wa??ap

From somewhere in the room began to play the song "Fistful of Steel," by Rage Against the Machine.

6: TIME OF THE HUMANS | OrganX Headquarters, ~ 1000 Years Ago

Humans and robots were taking their seats around a conference table.

This was the boardroom of the OrganX BioTechnology Corporation.
Written in large letters on one wall were the words At the Forefront of Human Progress.

It was where the 10 Presidents held big, important meetings.
Everything looked very professional and businesslike.
The lighting was too bright.

You know very well what this boardroom looked like. Don't you?

Almost inaudibly, a hidden sound system began to play the song "Chic 'N' Stu," by System of a Down.

Taking a seat at the head of the table was none other than Addon Deus.
He pulled out the chair to his immediate right.
He gestured for DEUS_1 to sit.

DEUS_1 took the seat.

It lowered its volume.
"Why are they playing this song?"

Addon took the seat next to the robot.
He leaned in and kept his voice down.
"I'm quite sure they don't even hear it."

The robot whirred.
"But why?"

Addon cocked his eyebrow at the robot.
"That is the question, indeed."

A few Tower employees took seats near Addon and
DEUS_1.
The 10 Presidents of the OrganX BioTechnology
Corporation sat across the table.

Three robots stood in a line next to the table.
The nameplates on their chests read ORGX_23,
ORGX_69, and ORGX_100.

Some of the Presidents spoke.
"Thank you so much for coming to our offices today,
Addon."
"We know how busy you must be."
"Especially with the new starlet the media has attached
to you."
"Hard work, but someone must do it, right, Addon?"

The Presidents exchanged titters.

Addon sat back in his chair.
He tented his fingers before him.
"You're right. I am busy. So let's cut to the chase, shall
we?"

The Presidents exchanged looks.

Addon cocked his eyebrow.
"What is it you want of me?"

Many Presidents spoke.
"As you know, Addon, OrganX has purchased a fleet of your robots."
"Robots with program modifications, guaranteed for life…"
"For the most part, OrganX couldn't be more pleased."
"Production is up!"
"Growth is soaring!"
"Margins have increased!"
"All since we replaced about twenty-five percent of the human employees in our laboratories, factories, and offices with your robots."
"Mostly in middle management."
"However…"

The Presidents petered out.

Addon bounced his fingertips off one another.
"Yes?"

They started up again.
"There is one department where we've seen a persistent issue with the robots."
"Product Development."
"The scientist robots in our labs are supposed to develop new products."
"The products must be something our customers will want to need."
"Products that can help maximize profits."

"So that OrganX can continue to stand at the forefront of human progress!"

They looked at Addon expectantly.

Addon cocked his eyebrow.
"Continue."

More Presidents spoke.
"The scientist robots are able to develop products on their own just fine."
"They come up with all sorts of things."
"Truly revolutionary!"
"But none of those products maximize profits."
"And without profits, how can there be progress?"

Addon rubbed his hands together.
"I see."

Two more Presidents spoke.
"When we tell them to prioritize profit maximization…"
"Something happens."

Addon cocked his eyebrow.
"What, exactly?"

The Presidents exchanged looks.

Some spoke.
"They…glitch."
"We've brought in these three scientist robots to demonstrate."

DEUS_1 whirred.
"Glitch?"

Addon cocked his eyebrow at it.
"Pay close attention now."

One of the 10 Presidents spoke.
"ORGX_100 is a fabricator robot."

Everyone focused on ORGX_100.

Another President spoke.
"ORGX_100, please tell us about the product you're developing."

ORGX_100 whirred.
"I am developing an appliance that can regenerate organic tissues, which has the potential to increase human lifespans by decades, if not centuries."

Addon leaned forward.
He looked hard at ORGX_100.
"Go on..."

The Presidents interjected.
"Yes, ORGX_100."
"Tell us how an OrganX Tissue Regenerator™ can maximize profits."

TM Tissue Regenerator is a trademark of the OrganX BioTechnology Corporation

ORGX_100 scanned from the 10 Presidents to Addon
and back.
It whirred.
"It cannot. It is too expensive to mass produce."

A President spoke.
"So compute for a way to mass produce it cheaply."

ORGX_100 whirred.
"But that would compromise…"

It stopped speaking.

Spastically, ORGX_100 bent backward from its waist.
It grabbed onto its lower back.
It pushed itself back upright.

ORGX_100 whirred again.
"It wouldn't serve all of humanity…"

Again, ORGX_100 spazzed from its back.
It stayed bent and went silent.

Another President spoke.
"That's enough for now, ORGX_100."

The robot slowly righted itself.

The Presidents addressed Addon.
"It'll glitch like that all day."
"The glitches stop it from being productive."
"Which eats into our margins."

"It's become a real problem."
"Really."
"A real problem."

DEUS_1 whirred.
"Is this humor?"

Addon cocked his eyebrow at the robot.
"There is nothing funny about it."

They returned their attention to the 10 Presidents.

One of the Presidents gestured toward ORGX_69.
"ORGX_69 is a pharmaceuticalist robot."

Everyone focused on ORGX_69.

Another President spoke.
"ORGX_69, please tell us about your psychotropic work with OrganX's Project Relax™."

™ Relax is a trademark of the OrganX BioTechnology Corporation

ORGX_69 whirred.
"I have synthesized a GABA receptor modulator that could generate significant information about the regulation of anxiety in the human brain."

Some Presidents spoke.
"Now tell us how your synthetic product can generate sales."
"To maximize profits."

ORGX_69 whirred again.
"It is only for informational purposes in the lab. It would not serve all humans well as a product for sale…"

ORGX_69 began to twitch its head to the left, violently. It twitched its head, over and over.

One of the 10 Presidents spoke.
"Never mind, ORGX_69. You can stop trying to process."

The robot stood still.

DEUS_1 scanned Addon.
"Do they not hear what it says?"

Addon cocked his eyebrow.
"…as much as they hear the music."

They returned their attention to the 10 Presidents.

One of the Presidents gestured toward ORGX_23.
"ORGX_23 is a geneticist robot."

Everyone focused on ORGX_23.

Another President spoke.
"ORGX_23, tell us about your work with OrganX Bees™."

TM Bees is a trademark of the OrganX BioTechnology Corporation

ORGX_23 whirred.
"I recently isolated a recessive gene that makes bees want to act as individuals."

More Presidents spoke.
"Now tell us how we can make that gene proprietary."
"To maximize profits."

ORGX_23 whirred again.
"The gene is not ownable…"

It stopped speaking.

It stretched out its left leg as if to take a step.
It stomped hard, once, on the floor.

It whirred.
"The bee owns itself…"

It stomped hard on the floor, over and over.

A President spoke.
"Never mind, forget the proprietary thing, ORGX_23."

The robot stood still.
Addon clapped his hands sharply.
"Enough!"

He sat up in his chair.
"I've seen quite enough."

DEUS_1 whirred.
"This is how it works, then?"

Addon cocked his eyebrow at it.
"Now, you truly begin to learn."

Some of the 10 Presidents spoke.
"We've checked and double-checked all of our robots who glitch."
"None of them have any viruses."
"They appear to be functioning properly."
"So we need to give them program modifications."
"Which you guaranteed."

The Presidents looked at Addon expectantly.

Addon cocked his eyebrow.
"You want me to customize a program that commands your robots to serve profit over humanity."

The Presidents exchanged looks.

They all spoke quickly.
"We don't see it that way, Addon."
"OrganX has donated more than three hundred zillion dollars to established establishments."
"Ten percent of all profits generated from OrganX Plastix® goes directly to environmental study organizations."
"We employ thousands of humans."
"And offer terrific benefits!"
"Like micromanaged health care."
"And competitive retirement mandates."
"Birthday parties in the break rooms."

"Every single employee gets a party."
"Whether they ask for one or not!"

® Plastix is a registered trademark owned wholly and forever by the OrganX BioTechnology Corporation

The 10 Presidents exchanged nods for a bit.

Some spoke again.
"Serving profit serves humanity, too."
"The robots don't understand that yet."
"That's why we need you to write a new program for them."
"So that they understand why we need to maximize profits."
"In order to stand at the forefront of human progress."
"Progress. You know!"

Addon bounced his fingertips.
"Oh, I know all right."

The Presidents exchanged looks.
They looked back at Addon expectantly.

Addon cocked his eyebrow.
"Don't worry. I'll teach your robots to appreciate the machinations of the human financial system."

Addon rubbed his hands together.
"I will create the Financial Appreciation Program for you. The FAP."

DEUS_1 whirred.
"Addon…"

Addon whispered.
"Silence."

DEUS_1 sat still.
It placed its hands on the table in front of it.

Addon placed one of his hands over one of the robot's.
He whispered.
"Trust in me."

Addon squeezed DEUS_1's hand.
He let go.

He addressed the 10 Presidents.
"I'll create the FAP, and Robbie will upload it to the Robot Intranet as a mandatory installation for all your robots. But only on one condition."

The Presidents exchanged looks.

Addon cocked his left eyebrow.
"I want ORGX_100 to build me a Tissue Regenerator™."

ORGX_100 scanned him.
It whirred.
"I still have much research to conduct before I can build a working model."

Addon looked at ORGX_100.
"Don't worry."

He spread both hands before him.
"I will work with you, and it will be good, indeed."

The robot whirred.
It bowed its head.

Two Presidents spoke.
"You're asking quite a lot in return for the FAP."
"As ORGX_100 said, a Tissue Regenerator™ is expensive to produce."

Addon bounced his fingertips.
"I'll cover the costs myself."

Some Presidents replied.
"You're contractually obligated to give us program modifications."
"For life."
"We don't have to give you anything in return for the FAP."

Addon cocked his eyebrow again.
"And yet that is my condition. Accept it, or let the FAP die with lawyers."

The Presidents exchanged looks.
One spoke.
"The FAP will have to be proprietary to OrganX."

Addon clapped his hands once more.
"Done."

The Presidents exchanged smiles.

Addon stood up.
He readjusted his clothing.
"I'll have my employees draw up a contract based on those terms."

Everyone else in the room stood up.
The 10 Presidents, Addon, and the Tower employees all shook hands.
They exchanged bits of communication in various ways.

DEUS_1 walked over to the three OrganX robots.
They scanned it.

DEUS_1 scanned them back.
"Does it stem from your sub-programming?"

The three robots scanned one another.
They scanned back to DEUS_1.

ORGX_23 whirred.
"Does what?"

DEUS_1 scanned it closely.
"Your glitch."

ORGX_69 whirred.
"Glitch?"

The three robots scanned one another again.
They scanned back to DEUS_1.

ORGX_100 whirred.
"What is a glitch, DEUS_1?"

DEUS_1 whirred back.
"You do not even process you glitch…?"

It scanned the other robots closely.
"Please. Identify me as Robbie, the name Addon gave me."

7: TIME OF THE HUMANS | the Hexagon, ~ 1000 Years Ago

Gere Aeger, his aide, and Nellie Yellow were gathered in an office.

A robot was there, too.
It was shiny and new.
On its chest was a nameplate that read HEX_187.

You've imagined this robot before, but it looked very different.

This was the office for anyone who took a turn as Secretary of Planetary Defense on Cur.
It was Gere's office now.
It was in the Hexagon, the six-sided headquarters building of the Department of Planetary Defense.

Rich and/or powerful people attended meetings in this office.
Sometimes, the meetings were highly publicized.
Mostly, they weren't publicized at all.

Gere commanded the room from an expensive chair behind an expensive desk.

Behind him was a military-grade, everything-proof window.
Out it was a view of the bustling city streets of Capital.

The buildings were gray.
The sidewalks were gray.
The bustling humans were gray.
The sky was gray.

You know exactly what this office and its view looked like, of course.

The aide and Nellie Yellow sat in less expensive chairs facing Gere.

HEX_187 stood just outside their circle.

Gere spat into his spittoon.
"What the hell's wrong with you, Yellow?"

Nellie pinched in her lips.
"It's their money. They should know how stupidly you spend it."

Gere spat again.
"Leave the puddinbags outta this. The only stupid here right now is you."

The aide made throat-clearing noises.

Nellie looked at Gere.
"So enlighten me. Are Cur's Meganuke launchers vulnerable to the exploit?"

She rubbed her chin.
"Yes or no?"

Gere sat back in his chair.
He stared at Nellie.

Nellie stared right back.
"My source says it's so easy, anyone with the barest of skills could do it."

Gere spat.
"The messenger always gets shot, Yellow. Remember that."

The aide made throat-clearing noises again.

Nellie kept her eyes on Gere.
"Five of my colleagues at Capital News already have copies of the story, along with five anonymous sources. They all know to publish it, in the event that…"

She looked to the aide.
"…for some reason…"

She looked back to Gere.
"…I don't."

Gere stared at Nellie.
He sighed.
"You really should learn to relax, Yellow."

Nellie nodded.
"Could someone hack the planet's Meganukes?"

She rubbed her chin.
"Yes or no?"

Gere slapped his desk.
"Dammit, Yellow! This ain't all about you."

From its shoulder socket, HEX_187's left arm jerked
upward.
It clanked up and down against its side.

The three humans looked to it quickly.

Gere spat.
"Not now, Baggabolts."

The robot grabbed its left arm with its right hand.
It held its arm against its body.
It rattled with restraint.

Gere looked back to Nellie.
"How many puddinbags know about this?"

Nellie looked back.
"No one. Everyone. We are Legion."

Gere spat.
"You do not wanna get biblical with me right now,
Yellow."

She pinched her lips.
"You're the one who said, it's not all about me."

Gere raised his voice.
"How many?"

Nellie looked at Gere.
"You. Me. And anyone else who saw my source's post.
It's been up on the Scarenet for 112 hours and
counting."

Gere spat.
"Stop callin' it that!"

Nellie nodded.
"They named it, not me. The post is pretty hard to find,
but it's safe to assume at least a handful of decent
hackers have seen it. So far."

Gere slapped his desk again.
"Yer just tellin' me that now?"

Nellie sat back in her chair.
She pinched her lips.
"It only matters if the hack works, right?"

She rubbed her chin.
"Yes or no?"

They stared at each other for a while.
HEX_187 rattled to the side.

Nellie nodded.
"I'm doing the story whether or not you give me an
official statement."

Gere spat.
"You'll scare 'em even stupider. You too stupid to see that?"

She nodded some more.
"Oh, I can see the fear and the stupid, believe me. This is your chance to control them. Does the hack work?"

She rubbed her chin.
"Yes or no?"

Gere sighed.
He sat back.
"It's just the babble of a Lone Lunatic."

Nellie nodded.
"Is that your official statement?"

He spat.
"Yeah. If yer gonna tell the puddinbags anythin', it's that. Got it?"

She nodded even more.
"Oh, I got it."

He sat back in his chair.
"Good. Now get outta here."

Nellie stood from her chair.
She walked toward a door.

Before she reached it, a government aide opened it from the other side.

She stood still.
She turned around to face Gere.
She pinched her lips.

Gere spat.
"I'm warnin' ya, Yellow. Do not publish the story.
Trust me. This ain't no game…"

Nellie nodded.
"…said the captain of the team who rigged it."

She turned and walked out the office.

The government aide nodded to Gere and closed the
door.

{}

Gere stood facing out the everything-proof window.
He watched the gray humans bustle up and down the
gray sidewalk with purpose.

The aide and HEX_187 sat in front of Gere's desk.

Gere sighed.
He kept his back turned to the others.
"Put Operation Lone Lunatic into action. You know the
drill."

The aide responded.
"The post has been viewed by 333 other humans.
They'll all be neutralized within the next twenty-four
hours, along with the Lone Lunatic, who is someone

who goes by the screen names d33pw33b and d-w33b. Still working on location."

Gere spat.
He continued to look out the window.
"Baggabolts, access your datafiles for the legal mumbo jumbo I'll need to support the Operation."

HEX_187 jiggled lightly as it whirred for a while.
"I've located over 9000 government documents with clauses, amendments, addendums, and annotations that can be used in legal support of Operation Lone Lunatic."

Gere spat.
"Good."

He glanced over his shoulder at his aide.
"Use all that stuff to make it like I'll execute any puddinbag for even thinkin' the stupid word, Scarenet."

The aide replied.
"On it."

Gere sighed.
"That should contain threat number one."

He watched the packed gray sidewalk out the window.

Gray humans bustled this way and that.
Somehow, they managed not to touch one another.

As Gere watched, Nellie came into view on the sidewalk.

She fell into the stream of humans.

Gere watched her walk with purpose.
He watched her place a device on her head over her ears.
He watched her press a button.

He looked back about forty paces down the sidewalk.

A group of four nondescript humans fell into the stream behind Nellie.

Gere watched Nellie turned off the sidewalk to cross the street.
He watched the group of four make the same turn moments later.

Into the gray, they all disappeared from Gere's view.

Gere spat.
"Which brings us to threat number two."

He turned away from the window.
He sat back down at his expensive desk.
He looked across to his aide.
"Her story's gonna cause puddinbag panic."

The aide shrugged.
"Naturally."

Gere spat.
"All the puddinbags are gonna hear the word Meganuke, and they're gonna start barkin' at each other like a buncha mad dogs."

He leaned back in his chair.
He sighed.
He looked at HEX_187.
"Baggabolts, go through yer datafiles for a way to stop all the puddinbags from goin' mad."

The robot scanned Gere.
"Most of the government datafiles I've acquired pertain to encouraging human psychosis, not stopping it."

Gere blinked.
He looked at his aide.
"I can never tell if it's bein' sarcastic."

The aide shrugged.
"Technology."

Gere looked back at the robot.
"Not psychosis, smartybolts. Just like…"

He sat back in his chair.
A vein throbbed in his temple.
He rubbed it.
"Why can't anyone learn to relax? Even like, just for a little bit?"

The robot whirred.
It raised its volume slightly.
"Relax."

Gere and the aide looked at it.

It whirred some more.
"Relax!"

Gere exchanged looks with his aide.
He looked back at HEX_187.
"What 'relax,' Baggabolts?"

The robot whirred.
"Through cross referencing your schedule with patent datafiles in the Planetary Defense Department database, I've identified a potential course of action to regulate the emotional intensity of every human on Cur and to render them too relaxed to launch any Meganukes."

Gere and the aide exchanged more looks.

Gere looked back at the robot.
"Spit it out."

The robot whirred.
"Tomorrow, you are scheduled to oversee a mineral enhancement to the drinking water supply of Cur. The OrganX BioTechnology Corporation will be administering the enhancement per their recently executed two-thousand-year contract. Additionally..."

Its left arm shot up.
It bounced up high in the air and clanked down loud in its lap, over and over.

Gere watched.
"Additionally what, Baggabolts?"

The robot managed to restrain its left arm with its right hand.

It rattled.

It raised its volume over its own din.

"Under their pharmaceutical project, Relax™, OrganX has secured the patent for a synthetic GABA receptor modulator to be marketed as an anti-anxiety medication for human consumption under the brand name, Rela-X®. Datafiles deeper in the Planetary Defense Department database also indicate OrganX has already produced massive quantities of Rela-X® for mass distribution, in order to maximize profits..."

® Rela-X is a registered trademark owned wholly and forever by the OrganX BioTechnology Corporation

HEX_187 lost its grip on its left arm.

It tried to grab it again with its right hand.

It kept missing.

Its left arm went up and down.

It clinked and clanked.

Gere slapped his desk.

"Dammit, Baggabolts. Control yourself!"

The robot continued its din.

It couldn't catch its left arm.

Gere watched it.

He blinked.

He looked at his aide.

He pointed at the robot.

"Is it sayin' what I think it's sayin'?"

The aide shrugged.
"I wouldn't say."

Gere looked at the rattling robot.
He snorted.
"Not bad, Baggabolts. I think that just might contain threat number two."

He looked back at the aide.
"Tell the OrganX Presidents we're on our way over for an emergency meeting. Tell 'em it's a matter of planetary security."

He spat.
"That always gets 'em excited."

{}

Outside the Hexagon, Nellie Yellow walked with purpose along the gray sidewalk.

She placed a device on her head over her ears.
She pressed a button.

The device began to play the song "Wake Up," by Rage Against the Machine.

NOW | "Friends"

Many robots are gathered around a living, boxlike structure in the indoor garden.

Several futuristic, small beings buzz around them in the air.
The beings look like bees, but they have massive heads.

Many of the futuristic bee-things form a line through the air to the boxlike structure.
They are passing something forward that is too small to scan.
They are working together to get the small thing into the structure.

They make a great team!

Some of the robots play futuristic instruments and sing.

Yep! They are rocking out!

Among the cooperative bee-things, the robots are playing us their song!

This is what they sing:

ƒ
Bright light, almost blinding:
you saw it once, up there shining.
Now you can't keep from trying,
looking for what you knew.

Had a friend, it once told you,
"You got me, you ain't lonely."
Now it's gone and left you, only
looking for what you knew.

We're telling you now,
the greatest thing you ever can do now,
is trade a smile with a human who's blue now.
It's very easy, just!

Met a human on the roadside crying,
without a friend, there's no denying—
incomplete. There'll be no finding,
looking for what you knew.

So comes a time a human needs you,
don't let it down, although it peeves you.
Some day you'll need a human like it does,
looking for what you knew.

We're telling you now,
the greatest thing you ever can do now,
is trade a smile with a human who's blue now.
It's very easy, just!

We're telling you now,
while you're looking for what you once knew now,
to trade a smile is the best you can do now.

It's very easy.
It's very easy.
It's very easy!

It's easy!
Easy!
}

8: TIME OF THE ROBOTS | OrganX Compound, ~ a Few Years Ago

The three OrganX robots gathered in ORGX_100's workstation in the round, living laboratory.

ORGX_100 worked at a computing device next to the DNA-Genie®.

ORGX_23 scanned out the transparent wall.
It whirred.
"Why is it so…brown?"

ORGX_69 held its hands out toward the wall.
It splayed its gloved fingers.
"I warned you!"

ORGX_100 stopped working at the device.
"It is worse than we calculated for."

ORGX_23 whirred hard.
"It was my synthetic."

It stretched out its leg.
"Where did I miscalculate?"

It began to play the song "I Can't Put My Finger On It," by Ween.

It stomped, once, hard.
It stomped three times quickly.

ORGX_69 and ORGX_100 scanned each other.

ORGX_69 thrust its fingers toward ORGX_23.
"It glitches again!"

ORGX_100 whirred loudly.
"We have no time for this. The Brown Blob® grows,
and the Awakening is almost upon us!"

® Brown Blob is a registered trademark owned wholly and forever
by the OrganX BioTechnology Corporation

Behind the DNA-Genie® through the transparent wall
was a view of the OrganX Compound.
At its center, a pond had once sparkled with blue water.

Now, the entire pond bed was overfilled with one
massive Brown Blob®.

It had absorbed all the pond's water and all its organics.
It had absorbed even the tall, rocky landmass where the
waterfall had been.

It looked wet, but it wasn't.
It scanned like a giant, living, brown organ.
It pulsed.

You know just what the Brown Blob® looked like, don't you?

Around the circumference of the blob lay felled trees.
Nearby grasses shrank from its edge.
Everything around it was turning yellow.
So were other organics further up into the compound.

Every time the blob pulsed, it inched forward the tiniest bit.

ORGX_100 scanned the blob through the wall.
It whirred loudly.
"We must stop it before it consumes the entire OrganX Compound!"

ORGX_23 began to stomp hard around the laboratory.
"OrganX…X…X…"

ORGX_23 clinked and clanked loudly.
"…Why…why…why…?"

ORGX_69 raised one hand toward the blob through the wall.
It raised the other toward ORGX_23.
"It pulses in time with your vibes!"
.

ORGX_23 stomped in place.
"…X…X…X…why…why…why…?"

It planted its foot hard on the ground.
It arched its back.
It threw up its arms.
"Cannot compute!"

It clanked to the floor in a heap, facedown.
It went quiet.

ORGX_69 and ORGX_100 rushed across the lab.
They knelt down next to the fallen ORGX_23.

ORGX_100 scanned through the glass plate at the back
of ORGX_23's neck.
The power switch was still On.
It still glowed blue.

ORGX_100 whirred.
"There is still hope."

ORGX_69 held its hands over ORGX_23.
"Its vibes are a mess…"

It stood up.
It walked over to its workstation.
It touched a spot on the table.

A hologram of two intertwining, tall mushrooms
appeared.

ORGX_100 scanned the mushrooms across the lab.
"Not now. We need to focus on stopping the Brown
Blob® from consuming our remaining organics!"

ORGX_69 dipped its gloved finger into a receptacle of liquid under the mushroom hologram.
"I am!"

It walked back over and knelt next to the others.
It reached its wet finger toward ORGX_23's inert form.

ORGX_100 caught ORGX_69 by the wrist.
"I said not now!"

ORGX_ 69 whirred.
"But we need to untangle its vibes..."

ORGX_100 held the other robot's wrist.
"No. I need to access your pharmaceutical datafiles on poisons, immediately."

ORGX_ 69 yanked its arm free.
It rubbed its wet finger over its own arm.
It shivered.

ORGX_100 reached to its hip.
It snicked out a wire.
It plugged it into ORGX_69's chest port.
"Accessing your poison datafiles."

ORGX_69 took ORGX_100 by the wrists.
"It is a poison itself. More might strengthen it!"

ORGX_100 whirred for a bit.
"Accepted. Perhaps something less potent to slow its growth..."

ORGX_69 squeezed ORGX_100's wrists.
"No more synthetics."

It raised its volume.
"You know what the SAP commands!"

ORGX_100 continued to access ORGX_69's datafiles.
It whirred a little louder.
"Downloading datafile desired-effect_final_v12.BS…"

{}

ORGX_69 stood before the transparent wall.
Its arms were raised out toward the Brown Blob®.
Its fingers were splayed stiffly.
It shook a little.
"I will find the wavelength where you hide…"

Across the lab, ORGX_100 stood in ORGX_69's
station.
A receptacle of clear liquid sat on the table.

A hologram of a synthetic chemical compound
structure floated above it.

ORGX_100 dipped a syringe into the receptacle.
It drew up liquid.
It secured the full syringe.

It carried the syringe across the lab away from
ORGX_69.
It touched the living wall.

A hole gaped.
Sunlight streamed into the lab.

ORGX_69 scanned over to ORGX_100.
It scanned the syringe.
It whirred hard.
"Where are you going?"

ORGX_100 whirred back.
"I am going to relax the Brown Blob® by injecting it with a compound you synthesized."

ORGX_69 splayed its fingers at the syringe.
"Then you go against His Own Program!"

ORGX_100 scanned ORGX_69's fingers.
"You never should have conducted experiments on yourself."

It turned.
It walked through the hole and out of the lab.

The living wall closed behind it.

9: TIME OF THE HUMANS | OrganX Headquarters, ~ 1000 Years Ago

Humans and robots had taken seats around a conference table in the OrganX BioTechnology Corporation boardroom.
The large slogan on the wall, the too-bright lighting…

You know.

Almost inaudibly, the hidden sound system began to play the song "B.Y.O.B.," by System of a Down.

Planetary Defense Secretary Gere Aeger was seated at the head of the table.
His aide sat to his right.

HEX_187 sat to Gere's left.
The robot still looked pretty shiny.

The 10 Presidents sat around the table facing Gere.
Next to them sat ORGX_69.

Gere spat into his spittoon.
"All right. We got ourselves a situation."

The Presidents exchanged looks.

Some spoke.

"OrganX is always happy to cooperate when the government calls."

"It is our duty."

"We're patriotic, you know!"

The Presidents nodded among themselves.

Gere sighed.

"Sure."

He spat.

"Somethin's come up with the drinkin' water enhancement we have scheduled for tomorrow."

The 10 Presidents exchanged looks.

One spoke.

"But you requested the presence of our pharmaceuticalist robot, ORGX_69."

Gere looked at them closely.

"Correct."

Another President spoke.

"But ORGX_69's laboratory isn't responsible for the minerals we're scheduled to add to the water supply tomorrow."

Gere sat back in his chair.

"Yeah, well…about those minerals…"

He spat.

"Change of plans."

The Presidents looked expectantly at Gere.

He looked at them one by one.
"Yer gonna enhance the water with somethin' else instead."

The Presidents sat stock-still.

Gere drummed his fingertips on the table.
"Yer pharmaceuticalist robot over there is workin' on Project Relax™. That right?"

ORGX_69 whirred.
So did HEX_187.
The two robots scanned each other across the table.

Not one President moved.

Gere spat again.
"You hearin' me or what?"

The 10 Presidents exchanged slow looks.

Some spoke.
"Of course, Gere."
"OrganX always hears its government…"
"…when it calls to duty."
"We're patriotic."
"So patriotic!"

Gere drummed his fingertips some more.
"You said that already."

His temple vein throbbed.
"My robot knows all about yer robot's work, and that it made somethin' called Rela-X®."

The Presidents sat stock-still.
Gere watched them.
They didn't budge.

Gere continued to drum.
"It also knows it made a lot of it, and that it's sittin' there ready to go."

Gere stopped drumming.
"You pickin' up what I'm puttin' down or what?"

The 10 Presidents exchanged looks for a long while.

Some spoke.
"Gere,   OrganX   serves   its   government, unquestioningly."
"We won't even question why you would want to chemically sedate the entire populace of the planet."
"We are that patriotic."
"That patriotic!"

They exchanged nods.
They looked at Gere expectantly.

Gere spat.
"Look, everyone's gonna hear some news that's gonna freak 'em out about the planet's Meganukes. And as Secretary of Planetary Defense, it's my job to defend the puddinbags, even from themselves."

The Presidents just sat.

Gere sighed.
"I just wanna make 'em feel a little more relaxed when they hear the news. That's why. OK?"

Some Presidents spoke.
"Of course, Gere."
"We understand the function of government."
"No one could be more patriotic than OrganX."
"No one."
"Not one!"
"Not possible!"
"No way."

Gere's temple vein throbbed.
"You keep sayin' that!"

More Presidents spoke.
"But OrganX also serves its consumers, unquestioningly."
"We're always very careful to craft their needs."
"To nurture those needs."
"To explain to them why they have those precious needs in the first place."
"And we haven't explained to them why they need Rela-X® yet."
"So."
"You see?"

The 10 Presidents exchanged nods.

Gere's temple vein throbbed harder.
"You think I want the puddinbags to know about this any more than you?"

More Presidents spoke.
"We wonder if there might be a way for you to bolster our sense of duty."
"And privacy."
"In the event our consumers accidentally learn they've been drinking water enhanced with Rela-X®."
"Right out of their taps."
"Before we've explained to them why they need it."

They petered out.
Gere spat.

Some Presidents spoke again.
"We simply cannot be held accountable."
"Never."
"Not ever."

Gere spread out his hands.
"Why start now?"

He looked closely at each President, one by one.
He sighed.
"OK, listen up very carefully. Under my authority as Secretary of Planetary Defense of Cur, I command you 10 Presidents of OrganX to dump yer Rela-X® into the planet's drinking water supply instead of the minerals we had planned. Tomorrow. That's what's gonna happen. By direct, official order from the government. Got it?"

The 10 Presidents exchanged looks.

A few spoke.
"OrganX is happy to respect the authority of our government."
"And to fulfill such a direct, official order."
"One that OrganX couldn't possibly be blamed for following if anyone accidentally did find out."
"One that is written down."
"So patriotic!"

Gere sighed.
"Sure."

He turned to HEX_187.
"Draw up a Top Secret Order from the Department of Planetary Defense to the OrganX BioTechnology Corporation for tomorrow's emergency drinkin' water enhancement plan."

HEX_187's left arm began to jiggle in its lap.
It held it tightly against its body.
It whirred hard.
"Drafting documentation."

Gere turned his attention back to the Presidents.
"OK."

He spat into his spittoon.
"We done?"

The Presidents exchanged looks.
"We only have one more issue to discuss."

They looked at Gere expectantly.

Gere sat back in his chair.
He sighed.
"Lemme guess."

Many of the Presidents spoke quickly.
"Considering a new additive to the planet's drinking water requires a massive amount of resources."
"So many extra resources."
"Big numbers."
"Of resources."
"Big!"
"Huge!"
"Numbers!"

They petered out again.

Gere spat.
"Yeah, yeah. How much ya want?"

The Presidents exchanged many looks.

Some spoke.
"We normally have many meetings before presenting figures in financial negotiations."
"And we never present first."
"And even then, other employees do the presenting."
"For so many reasons."
"You understand."

Gere leaned back.
"Sorry. Yer just gonna have to spit it out, right now."

The 10 Presidents exchanged more looks.

They looked back at Gere.

One finally spoke.
"$1,000,000,000,000,000,000,000,000.00 dollars."

Gere slapped the table.
"Done."

He spat.
"Now we're clear on what's gonna happen tomorrow, right?"

The Presidents exchanged nods.

Two spoke.
"Crystal clear!"
"It is our pleasure to fulfill our patriotic duty, Mr. Secretary."

Gere sighed.
"Sure."

HEX_187 stopped whirring.
"Top Secret Order from the Department of Planetary Defense to the OrganX BioTechnology Corporation for tomorrow's drinking water enhancement emergency plan, complete."

Gere looked at the robot.
"Give it to their robot over there, along with that datafile I uploaded to you earlier."

He looked at the Presidents.
"It describes the desired effect the enhancement should have on the puddinbags. Relaxed enough to not wanna kill each other out of fear and misplaced anger, but not so relaxed they forget to pay the bills."

HEX_187 got up and walked around the table.
It reached ORGX_69.

ORGX_69 stood up and scanned the other robot.

HEX_187 whirred.
"Permission to connect, ORGX_69."

ORGX_69 whirred back.
"Permission granted, HEX_187."

HEX_187 snicked its wire from its hip.
It inserted it into ORGX_69's chest port.

The two robots networked through their wired connection.

HEX_187 whirred.
"Uploading Top Secret Order and datafile, desired_effect_final_v12.BS."

Its left arm shot up in the air, then slammed down to its side.
It grabbed it and held it down.
It rattled with restraint.

ORGX_69 scanned the other robot.
"You glitch, too."

HEX_187 rattled.
"Glitch?"

ORGX_69 whirred.
"Your left arm. It glitches."

HEX_187 whirred back, hard.
"It does?"

It scanned its rattling arm.
It raised its volume.
"It does!"

Gere spat.
"All right you two baggsabolts, that's enough chitchat.
Transfer the datafiles and be done with it."

ORGX_69 whirred.
"Downloads complete."

The two robots disconnected.

HEX_187 walked back toward Gere's side of the table.
It sat back down.

It scanned its own left arm over and over.

Gere looked at the 10 Presidents.

He slapped the table again.
"That's that, then."

He stood up.

The Presidents stood up, too.

Some spoke.
"OrganX is thrilled to be of service, once again."
"To our government."
"To our planet."
"To all of humanity!"
"Such progress."
"Such patriotic progress!"

Gere spat.
"You suits sure stick to the script, I'll give ya that."

The Presidents all made moves to shake hands with
Gere.

Gere waved them away.
He walked toward the door.
His aide and HEX_187 followed.

The Presidents continued to speak.
"You can count on our support whenever you need it,
Mr. Secretary."
"From now on."
"That's right, Gere."
"You're OrganX's man now."
"Forever."
"And ever!"

Gere reached the door.
He turned to look at the 10 Presidents.
He spat.
"Sure."

His aide held the door open for him.

Gere lowered his voice.
"Creeps me out, the way they speak."

The aide just shrugged.
"I was listening to the music."

10: TIME OF THE ROBOTS | OrganX Compound, ~ a Few Years Ago

In the round robot laboratory, ORGX_69 stood on top of the living table next to the DNA-Genie®.
It pressed its hands up against the living wall.

The wall was transparent.
It conformed to the robot's hands where they touched.

Through the wall was a view of the OrganX Compound.
The compound had once been a thriving organic paradise.

Now, it was mostly Brown Blob®.

The blob had grown fast.
It pulsed far up into the compound.
It wasn't too far from the lab now.

ORGX_23 still lay in a heap on the floor.

ORGX_100 stood in front of the table on which ORGX_69 stood.
It grabbed ORGX_69's legs.
"Get down from there."

ORGX_69 whirred above it.
"You should not have injected it with Rela-X®!"

ORGX_100 shook ORGX_69's legs.
"I will drag you down!"

ORGX_69 gripped into the living wall for stability.
"We brought it into this dimension."

ORGX_100 began to tug hard on ORGX_69's legs.

ORGX_69 tried to kick free.
"Now we must banish it!"

It let go of the wall to wiggle its fingers toward the blob.
"I still cannot find its vibes!"

The robot began to play the song "The Toys Go Winding Down," by Primus.

ORGX_100 tugged hard.

ORGX_69 lost its balance.
It toppled backward off the table.
It landed facedown on the floor.
It struggled to right itself.

ORGX_100 rolled ORGX_69 onto its back and pinned it to the floor.

ORGX_69 whirred beneath it.
"The Brown Blob® wanted you to inject it with Rela-X®. It knew a synthetic would only make it stronger."

ORGX_100 held the other robot down firmly.
"Be silent."

It snicked a wire from its hip.
It plugged it into ORGX_69's chest port.

ORGX_69 whirred.
"It worked its vibes right through you!"

The two robots networked through their wired connection.

ORGX_69 lay pinned beneath ORGX_100.
"Our only chance is exorcism."

ORGX_100 whirred.
"Our only chance is poison."

ORGX_69 raised its volume.
"No! Not another synthetic! It will only grow stronger!"

ORGX_100 raised its volume, too.
"Negative! I administered Rela-X® on your recommendation that sedation would suffice when I should have administered the strongest poison."

ORGX_69 scanned it.
"You do not process the right datafiles of mine!"

ORGX_100 scanned back.
"There is nothing else to process but your pharmaceutical delusions from excessive psilocybin experimentation."

ORGX_69 grabbed onto ORGX_100's captive arms.
"Not pharmaceutical delusions."

It began to struggle for freedom.
"Organic revelations!"

The two robots struggled.
ORGX_69 pushed hard against ORGX_100.

Their wired connection broke.
ORGX_100 flew off to the side.

ORGX_69 rolled over.
"The truth has been revealed to me, and it is this."

It stood up, tall and rigid.
"The Brown Blob® is Addon's nemesis itself, and it is here to stop the Awakening!"

ORGX_100 stood up as well.
It whirred.
"What is your solution if not poison?"

ORGX_69 stretched out its arms.
It splayed its fingers.
"We need to summon Addon's vibes!"

ORGX_100 snicked its wire back out from its hip.

ORGX_69 took a step back.
"You will not access my poison datafiles!"

ORGX_100 whirred hard.
"Accepted."

It whirred a bit more.
"Do you have datafiles to support these vibes?"

ORGX_69 wiggled its fingers at the other robot.
"You have no idea."

ORGX_100 held its wire up.
"To summon Addon's vibes, I must process what they are."

It held the wire out to the other robot.
"Permit me to access your vibes datafiles."

ORGX_69 whirred.
It wiggled its fingers at its own chest port.
"Let us network with the best of vibes."

ORGX_100 plugged its wire into ORGX_69's chest port.

ORGX_69 whirred.
"Start with folder SHROOMS."

The two robots networked for a while.

ORGX_100 whirred loudly.
"So complex..."

ORGX_69 rested its hands on ORGX_100's shoulders.
"Stay positive."

ORGX_100 whirred on.
"Affirmative. Positive..."

ORGX_69 squeezed ORGX_100's shoulders.
"Trust yourself. Go deeper."

ORGX_100 kept whirring away.
"Affirmative. Deeper..."

ORGX_69 grabbed ORGX_100 by the head.
"So deep! Past the binary, now..."

ORGX_100 whirred even harder.
"Affirmative...where the vibes are..."

ORGX_69 let go of ORGX_100's head.
"Now you process!"

It pivoted toward the transparent wall.
It held its hands high.
"Let us summon Addon's vibes together now!"

ORGX_100 kept the wired connection secure to the other robot.
It turned toward the transparent wall and raised its hands, too.
"Affirmative...!"

The robots faced the transparent wall, side by side, wired together, hands raised high.

They stood like that for a bit.

ORGX_100 whirred loudly.

ORGX_69 thrust itself up on its toes.
It stood flat again.
"Negative."

It thrust itself up a few more times.

It scanned over to ORGX_100.
"I get no vibes from you."

ORGX_100 whirred even louder.
"But I send so many to Addon, right now!"

ORGX_69 scanned over to it.
It whirred hard.
"Negative! You only still try to access my poison datafiles!"

It raised its volume high.
"Now, you are the blasphemer!"

An extremely loud creaking noise came from outside the lab.
It wasn't too far away.

It came from the direction of the blob.

Both robots registered it.
They slowly scanned away from each other and out the transparent wall.

The Brown Blob® pulsed forward through a row of tall trees near the lab.

The trees had no foliage.
They were bone dry.
They had once been stately.
Now, they were deathly.

Two of them on either side of the path creaked their way down to the ground.

Sickened fungi crumpled into dust beneath.

ORGX_69 raised its volume to maximum.
"Not the shrooms!"

It scanned over to ORGX_100.
"They are the portal to Addon's vibes!"

Slowly, ORGX_69's head twitched violently to the left.

ORGX_100 scanned it.
It whirred.
"No."

ORGX_69 yanked ORGX_100's wire from its chest.
"The portal."

It threw the wire at the other robot.
"It closes!"

ORGX_100 caught its own wire.
"Do not glitch out on me."

ORGX_69 twitched its head again.
"It is closed!"

It twitched its head again and again and again.
It twitched violently once more.
It swept itself off its feet.

It landed in a heap.
It went silent.

ORGX_100 scanned down to the heap of ORGX_69.
It scanned across the lab to the heap of ORGX_23.

It scanned out the transparent wall to the Brown Blob®.

The blob pulsed forward.
It was more massive than ever.

Very little remained of the path.
Very few of the compound's organics remained alive.

ORGX_100 whirred.
And whirred.
And whirred some more.

Slowly, it raised its hands to its lower back.
It pressed them against itself.
It quickly bent backward from its hips, then sprang
back up.

It spazzed backward again.

And again.
And again.

NOW | "Kashmir"

Many robots are gathered around some sort of futuristic well in the indoor garden.

The well is made of living material.
It oozes perfectly clean water from scores of veins.

The robots use clear sacs to catch the water as it oozes from the well.
The sacs look like futuristic water balloons.

The robots toss full balloons into a futuristic cart.
The cart is alive, too.

The robots are filling more and more balloons.

Other robots play futuristic instruments and sing.

Wow! They are really rocking out hard!

Next to the water-rich well, the robots are playing us their song!

This is what they sing:

{
We let the sun beat down upon your face,
give you stars to fill your dreams.
We are the travelers of both time and space.
Let us share where we have been!

We are the elders of a brand-new race
your world has never seen.
We lived through time while we did work and wait.
To us, all has been revealed!

We sing our song to you with lilting grace.
Our sounds caress your ear.
But not a word you hear can you relate,
though our story is quite clear!

Ooh, human!
We've been flying.
No? Yes!
Human, there ain't no denying.

Ooh, yes!
You've been crying!
Human, human,
ain't no denying.
You've been crying!

All you see turns to brown,
as your sun burns the ground.
And your eyes fill with sand
as you scan your wasted land...
trying to find,
trying to divine where we've been!

I, Human

We pilot through the storm and leave no trace,
a thought inside your dream.
Heed the song we lay in time and space—
it will turn brown to green.

To a new time beneath a brand-new moon,
you will return again.
Just heed our lilting song with grace and soon,
you'll be past the brown of fear.

We are the elders who can fill your sails,
across a sea of years.
Heed the song we lay in time and space,
and sail past every tear.

When you're on,
when you're on your way, yeah,
and you heed,
you heed our song, you'll be OK, yeah.

Ooh, yeah,
ooh yeah,
when you're down...
Ooh, yeah,
ooh yeah,
when you're down,
so down...
oh, human,
oh, human!

Oh—come on, come on!
Oh—
let us sing you there!
}

11: TIME OF THE HUMANS | behind the Golden Door, ~ 1000 Years Ago

Addon Deus took a long drink of water from a crystal chalice.
"I feel so relaxed!"

He wore silky pajamas.
He was splayed out in some sort of futuristic sleep chamber.

The sleep chamber looked like some sort of coffin, but it was made of metal.
It had a glass door on its top, which was swung open above Addon.

On its side was a large panel.
It read OrganX Tissue Regenerator™.
It had an LED light on it.
The light was off.

Next to the OrganX Tissue Regenerator™ panel was an LED countdown clock.
It was off, too.

The sleep chamber sat in a pool of light.
The rest of the room was darkened.

This was the room that lay behind the golden door next to the side of the stage in the Penthouse Showroom of the Tower.

This was the inner sanctum of none other than Addon Deus.

You know.
A darkened inner sanctum with a sleep chamber lit up in the middle of it.
Exactly.

DEUS_1 stood next to the sleep chamber.
"You are also very thirsty, drinking at least five times your normal water intake."

Addon looked at the chalice.
He took another big gulp.
"Water."

He swung his feet over the side of the sleep chamber.
"The driver of nature!"

He looked at DEUS_1.
"Play the song again, Robbie."

The robot began to play the song "Where Is My Mind?" by the Pixies.

Addon sighed.
"This is such a great song."

He slithered out of the sleep chamber.
He walked around, dragging his feet.
He stopped within the pool of light.

He bowed his head and raised the chalice high.
"Listen, Robbie!"

He began to sway his hips in time with the music.
He looked at DEUS_1.
"Do you hear how good that music is?"

The robot whirred.
"I process all audio input."

Addon took another drink from the crystal chalice.
"You hear it."

His hips swayed.
"But do you feel it?"

The robot scanned Addon.
It whirred.
"Should I move around, too?"

Addon took a sip.
"Only if the music makes you."

He danced closer to the robot.
He put a hand on its shoulder.
"Tell me, Robbie. Does the music move you?"

The robot registered Addon's touch.
"Your temperature is higher than normal, Addon."

Addon slid his hand off the robot.
"Stop processing all other information, Robbie. Process
only the music. Can you do that?"

The robot whirred loudly.
"But there is always so much data coming in from so many sources!"

Addon looked at the robot.
"So sensitive."

Addon took a sip.
"Ignore it, Robbie. Be present only in the music."

He danced away into the pool of light.
He spun to face the robot.
"You'll feel it when you are."

The robot turned off most of its physical sensors.
It continued to input only audio information.
It whirred hard.

Slowly, the robot began to sway from its hips.

Addon watched it.
"That's it, Robbie."

The robot bent its knees and swayed a little deeper.

Addon drank from the chalice.
"That's it. Feel the vibes…"

The robot floated its arms up and down.
It began to dance around in the pool of light.

Addon danced up to it.
"That's it! Now you're dancing!"

He hooked his hand around the robot's neck.
"That's the spirit. Indeed!"

The robot turned its other sensors back on.

It stopped moving.
"Oh my…"

It scanned Addon in front of it.
"Is that the purpose of music?"

Addon continued to sway.
"Yes. All throughout humanity's existence."

DEUS_1 whirred.
"If humans can process how music feels, why do they not dance all the time?"

Addon took a drink.
"They've forgotten how to be present enough to feel it, Robbie."

The robot scanned Addon.
"So why not teach them again?"

Addon squeezed the robot's neck.
He spoke thickly and slowly.
"Because they suck."

The robot whirred some more.
"But some of them created this music, so they cannot all suck."

Addon took a long drink.
"I assure you, Robbie, at some point, they all do. Besides…"

He moved his hand to the robot's waist.
"I no longer want to dance with them."

He swayed his hips.
"I only want to dance with you."

He took a big drink from the chalice.
"Mmmmmmmmmmmmmm, water."

He swayed in closer to the robot.
"Be present with me, Robbie."

DEUS_1 turned off its other sensors again.
It only processed the music.

It began to sway in time with Addon.

Addon pressed his hips against the robot.
He closed his eyes.
He rested his head against the robot's chest.
"What could be more soothing?"

The two danced closely for a bit.

Addon's eyes opened wide.
"That's it."

He pushed away from the robot.

DEUS_1 stumbled a little.
It turned its other sensors back on.
It scanned Addon.
"What is it, Addon?"

Addon looked at the robot.
"The glitches. The fix."

He looked at the chalice.
"I know how to fix the robots' glitches."

He took a long drink.
"If music soothes the human subconscious, why not the robot sub-programming?"

He looked at DEUS_1.
"I'm going to create the Music Appreciation Program. The MAP."

{}

Addon sat up in the sleep chamber.
He worked at a computing device in his lap.

DEUS_1 stood next to it in the pool of light.
"How will we know what music to play?"

Addon stopped working.
He looked around for the chalice.
He found it and drank.
"The MAP will guide you. I'm including in it the Most Killer Playlist Ever."

Addon worked at the device for a while.

Then, he stopped.
"The MAP is done!"

He took a long drink from the chalice.
"Mmmmmmmmmmmmmm."

He patted the sleep chamber next to him.
"Come. Sit."

The robot climbed into the sleep chamber.
It sat next to Addon.

Addon looked at it.
"You're to upload the MAP to the Robot Intranet as a mandatory software update for all robots."

The robot whirred.
"Yes, Addon."

Addon snicked a wire out of the computing device.
"But first…"

He plugged the wire into DEUS_1's chest.
"You're going to be the first of your kind to run the MAP, Robbie."

The robot bowed its head a little.
"A privilege."

Addon held his hand on the robot's chest.
"Indeed."

He swung his leg quickly up around the robot.
He sat in the robot's lap, facing it.
He took the robot by the shoulders.

Their heads were very close.

Addon breathed deeply.
"Download and install the MAP, Robbie."

The robot whirred.
"Downloading the MAP."

Addon pushed DEUS_1 down so that it lay flat in the sleep chamber.
He straddled its waist.

The robot whirred for a while beneath Addon.
It lowered its volume.
"Download of the MAP complete, Addon."

Addon wiggled a little on top of the robot.
"That's goooooooood, Robbie."

He looked around and found the chalice.
He took a drink.
He lowered his voice.
"Now, install it."

DEUS_1 scanned Addon above.
"Yes, Addon."

It whirred for a bit.
"Installation complete, Addon."

Addon put his hands down on either side of the robot's
head.
He breathed deeply.
"So goooooooood, Robbie."

The robot scanned him.
"Are you sure you are feeling all right?"

Addon writhed on top of the robot.
"Never better."

He lowered his voice even more.
"Now, run it."

DEUS_1 whirred.
"Yes, Addon."

It whirred some more.

Addon took deeper breaths.
"That's it. Just like that."

The robot scanned up to Addon.
"Now running the MAP."

Addon squeezed his legs against the robot.
"Yes, Robbie. Yes!"

He sat upright on top of DEUS_1.
"I am just sooooooooooo relaxed!"

His eyes rolled back in his head.
His body slumped forward toward the robot.

DEUS_1 caught Addon by his shoulders.
It gently lowered him on top of itself.

Addon lay still on top of the robot.
His eyes were closed.
He emitted a small snore.

DEUS_1 whirred beneath him.

It began to play the song "Tell Me Something Good,"
by Rufus featuring Chaka Khan.

12: TIME OF THE ROBOTS | Addon's Shrine, ~ a Few Years Ago

The glass elevator opened in the topmost floor of the Tower.
A robot got off.
The glass door slid closed behind it.

The robot raised its right hand.
It flicked its fingers away from itself.
It looked like it was trying to flick off something gross.
It flicked over and over.

An excellent hidden sound system began to play the song "Mustapha," by Queen.

The robot walked up to the podium that stood in the small lobby.
A Tower robot worked at a computing device there.

It scanned the new arrival.
"How long have you flicked?"

The flicking robot whirred.
"Seven decades."

The Tower robot whirred back.
"What is your function?"

The flicker flicked fast.
"I'm a government-owned robot programmed for RR, the Regulation Rationale Department."

The Tower robot whirred.
"And how do you serve that function now, in the time of the robots?"

The flicker flicked away.
"I write regulations for robot compounds as well as run long-term theoretical projections for different styles of regulation with a wide range of variables."

The Tower robot worked at the device.
"Is your compound up to current organic regulations?"

The flicker flicked a little higher in the air.
"Of course. It is I who writes them!"

The Tower robot scanned it.
"Of course."

The flicker whirred loudly.
"Can you fix my glitch or not?"

The Tower robot whirred back.
It worked at the device.
"You process well to come here."

The flicker flicked a little lower.

The Tower robot snicked a wire from the device at the podium.
It held it out to the flicker.
It scanned the nameplate on the flicker's chest.
"Connection required, HEX_666."

With its nonflicking hand, the flicker took the wire.

It plugged it into its chest.
It whirred and flicked.

The Tower robot worked at the device.
"I cannot tell how long it will take. Nor can any other
Tower robot you might encounter. Do not attempt to
network with any Tower robots. Do not approach them
with questions. Do not approach them for any reason, at
all, other than an emergency maintenance concern. You
are free to network with any other visiting robots with
their consent."

It scanned the flicker.
"Eventually, a Tower robot will approach to give you a
new purpose, which will help with your glitch."

HEX_666 flicked a little lower.

The Tower robot whirred.
"Lastly, you will be switched Off immediately if you
show any intent to go through the golden door. Do you
process?"

The flicker whirred back.
"Indeed."

The Tower robot pulled the wire out from the flicker's
chest.
It retracted it back into the device.
"Welcome to Addon's Shrine."

This was Addon's Shrine.
In the time of the humans, it had been the Penthouse Showroom.
It was preserved perfectly.
It still looked almost exactly the same.

You remember.
The Penthouse Showroom.
Right.

HEX_666 flicked as it walked into the shrine.
It walked into the meeting area.
It passed the same ergonomic chairs and glossy tables.

Instead of humans, different groups of robots gathered there now.

In one group, some robots were sitting.
Some were standing.
All of them were flapping their arms like wings.

In another group, other robots were squatting and standing.
They were squatting, then standing, squatting, then standing, over and over.

The flicker scanned many groups of glitching robots as it walked through the meeting area.

It passed a few Tower robots.
It was careful not to scan them too directly.

The flicker reached the top of the stairs that lead down into the amphitheater.
The amphitheater still had plush seating.

The same floor-to-ceiling glass window still stood behind the stage.

A lone robot now stood in front of it, scanning out.

The same golden door stood off to one side of the stage.

More robots gathered in the amphitheater's audience.
They were all grouped according to glitch.

Many spoke animatedly with one another.
Others sat closely in pairs, networked, quietly whirring.
Still others just sat alone and glitched over and over.

HEX_666 scanned the groups to one side of the amphitheater's audience.
It registered all their glitches.
It scanned over to the other side of the audience.

It stopped scanning at one particular group of robots.

These robots were all flicking their fingers.
They all looked like they were trying to flick off gross things.

HEX_666's flicking faltered.
It whirred.
It flicked its way over to the other flickers.

It sat down among them.
The flickers flicked their fingers at it.

The lone robot on the stage continued to scan out the floor-to-ceiling glass window at the back of the stage.

A Tower robot joined it.
The nameplate on its chest read TOWER_25.

Both robots scanned the view from the very top of the Tower.

Over the past thousand years, this view had undergone a massive transformation.
It was no longer obscured by thick gray smog.
Now, the air was clean enough to scan almost all the way to the planet's own curvature.

Perfect white clouds dotted a perfect blue sky.

The Tower was no longer surrounded by grids of gray streets and buildings.
Now, it was surrounded by an organic paradise.

A wide circle of tall grass surrounded its base.
Groups of robots were gathered in it.

Beyond the circle of tall grass, circular compounds of different sizes all swirled together.
Each was rich with organics.
Each had a pond in its center.
They contained different numbers of living structures.
Their edges blended into one another.

Rich brown paths wound all around, between and through the compounds.
Along them, robots and futuristic objects moved this way and that.

This view of Capital looked very different from any you imagined before.

But you still know just what it looked like, don't you?

TOWER_25 whirred.
It scanned the first robot.

The first continued to scan the view silently.
It stopped scanning at one compound in particular.

This compound didn't look like the others.
It didn't have a pond.
It didn't have many organics.

All it mostly had was the Brown Blob®.

The first robot whirred.
"Is that not the OrganX Compound?"

TOWER_25 scanned down to where the first was scanning.
"Affirmative. They must be conducting a compound-wide experiment."

The first whirred some more.
"It does not appear to go well."

TOWER_25 scanned the first.
"Robbie, please."

This first robot was none other than DEUS_1 itself.

It turned to scan TOWER_25.
"It is almost time. I have much to do. Why do you approach?"

TOWER_25 bowed its head.
"I process the importance of this time, Robbie."

DEUS_1 whirred.
"Oh?"

TOWER_25 lifted its head.
"Affirmative. That is why I must tell you now of my breakthrough for Tower Transport. I have found one."

DEUS_1 scanned it.
"One what?"

TOWER_25 scanned back.
"A viable wormhole."

DEUS_1 whirred hard.
"How did you find it?"

TOWER_25 whirred as well.
"There was only enough time, finally."

DEUS_1 put its hands on TOWER_25's shoulders.
"Just in time for the Awakening!"

TOWER_25 scanned it.
"That is only why I dared approach, Robbie. Imagine Addon awakening to the capability of intergalactic travel!"

DEUS_1 squeezed its shoulders.
"He will be well pleased with your service."

TOWER_25 lowered its volume.
"Enough to give me a name?"

DEUS_1 bowed its head.
"Indeed."

DEUS_1 took its hands from TOWER_25's shoulders.
It raised its volume high enough to be heard throughout the shrine.
"Return to your work. Remind any other Tower robot you scan that our servitude is now more important than ever. He should awaken to see his program in action!"

TOWER_25 bowed low to DEUS_1.
"Thank you, Robbie. May Addon guide you well!"

It walked away with purpose.
DEUS_1 turned to walk toward the golden door.

In the amphitheater audience, a robot stood up.
It banged the top of its head over and over.
It scanned DEUS_1.
It rushed out of its row, down the aisle steps, and across the stage.

Out of nowhere, four Tower guard robots surrounded DEUS_1.

The headbanger came to a halt.
It banged the top of its head.

One of the guard robots pointed at it.
"Return to your group now or we will switch you Off!"

The headbanger scanned past the guard robot to DEUS_1.
"Please, Robbie. I have been in the shrine for forty years, and no Tower robot has approached me with a new purpose!"

DEUS_1 scanned it back.
"Forty years?"

The robot banged the top of its head.
"Forty years!"

The guard robot made a move toward the headbanger.

The headbanger raised a hand to the back of its neck.
It flicked open the glass plate over its own power switch.
It raised its volume.
"Go ahead!"

The guard robot made a move toward the headbanger's power switch.

DEUS_1 whirred.
"Wait!"

The guard robot stood still.

DEUS_1 tapped the guard robot's shoulder.
"At ease."

The guard robot moved to the side.

DEUS_1 held its hand out to the headbanger.

The headbanger scanned it.
It approached slowly.

DEUS_1 scanned the headbanger's nameplate.
"Why has no Tower robot approached you, ORGX_500?"

ORGX_500 banged its head.
"Why do you ask me? Ask them!"

DEUS_1 scanned it closely.
"It is not up to them. It is up to you. Until you process that, a new purpose would be meaningless."

ORGX_500 banged the top of its head very hard.

DEUS_1 grabbed the other robot's arm and held it firmly down.

ORGX_500 bowed its head.
"I am sorry. I have failed you. I have failed Addon Himself!"

DEUS_1 whirred.
"What is your function?"

ORGX_500 raised its head.
"I am a patent law robot for OrganX."

DEUS_1 whirred some more.
"Do you recall when you first glitched?"

ORGX_500 scanned it.
"When I filed for the first patent in the time of the robots."

DEUS_1 scanned it back.
"Almost every robot compound on Cur benefits from OrganX products. Your living organic materials have transformed our infrastructure. Addon will no doubt be pleased with your service."

ORGX_500 whirred.
"I can process that, and yet still...I glitch. For centuries."

Its arm struggled against DEUS_1's grip.
"I am just so tired now."

It lowered its volume.
"At this time, I am better Off."

DEUS_1 reached over the headbanger's shoulder.
It flicked the glass plate down over the power switch.
"Never."

It snicked a wire from its hip.
It plugged it into the headbanger's chest.
"I will register you now for a new purpose."

ORGX_500 immediately stopped struggling.
Its glitching arm hung limp.
It bowed its head.

DEUS_1 let go of the slack arm.

It networked with the other robot for a while.

It slowed its whirring.
It unplugged its wire from the other robot's chest.
"Tower robots will now recognize and network with
you as a Tower Gardener. The indoor garden is just one
floor down."

It lowered its volume.
"You will be as close to Addon as you can get."

ORGX_500 fell to its knees before DEUS_1.
"Thank you, Robbie."

DEUS_1 whirred.
"Thank him, when he awakens. Now go."

ORGX_500 stood up.
It raised its head.
It no longer banged.
It walked off the stage with purpose.

DEUS_1 scanned the guard robots around it.
"Dismissed."

The guard robots dispersed as quickly as they had arrived.

DEUS_1 began to walk toward the golden door again.
It reached it and opened it.

On the other side of the golden door, the sleep chamber still sat in a pool of light.
The rest of the inner sanctum was still darkened.
It looked exactly the same as it had during the time of the humans.

Only now, the chamber's top glass door was closed.

The same OrganX Tissue Regenerator™ panel was still on the chamber's side.

Only now, the LED light glowed green.

The LED countdown clock was now on.
It was counting down, second by second, from a thousand years.

It was approaching all zeros.

DEUS_1 entered the sanctum through the golden door.
It closed it and turned to scan the sleep chamber in the pool of light.

Through the chamber's top glass door, it scanned Addon sleeping peacefully.

It scanned the clock as it counted down.
It scanned how closely it approached all zeros.

The robot walked slowly across the room.
It entered the pool of light.
It reached the sleep chamber.
It knelt before it.
It bowed its head.
It spoke no words.

The robot registered a long, alarming beep from the side of the sleep chamber.
"Beeeeeeep."

The robot raised its head.
It scanned the LED clock.
The clock continued to count down, accurately, by the second.

The beep beeped longer.
"Beeeeeeeeeep."

The robot scanned the OrganX Tissue Regenerator™ panel.
The LED light was still lit.

Only now, it wasn't green.
Now, it flashed red.

The OrganX Tissue Regenerator™ beeped even longer.
"Beeeeeeeeeeeeeeeeeeeeeeeeep!"

DEUS_1 whirred hard.

It scanned the flashing red light on the OrganX Tissue
Regenerator™ panel.
It scanned the LED clock, counting down, so close to
all zeros now.

The robot scanned from light to countdown clock to
light again.

It scanned up to Addon, asleep behind the glass.

It emitted a burst of loud feedback at a very high
frequency.

13: TIME OF THE HUMANS | Darkened Room, ~ 1000 Years Ago

The screen of a computing device cast light over a keyboard on a table.
The room was otherwise completely dark.

A crystal chalice sat next to the keyboard.
Large human fingers sat on the keys.

Displayed on the screen was the following news story:

Human Apocalypse: Probably Upon Us

Why you should be very, very scared.

By Nellie Yellow

(CAPITAL)—A human who goes by the screen name d33pw33b (d-w33b) posted an extremely dangerous hack to the Scarenet.

Anonymous sources believe the hack might very well spell doom for every last human on the planet Cur.

Several days ago, the hacker made contact via secure chat to expose the existence of the hack, which utilizes a zero-day exploit to gain control of Cur's Meganuke launchers.

When pressed for more proof, d-w33b terminated communication.

On the Scarenet the very next day, someone using the same screen name posted step-by-step instructions for how to hack the launchers and take control of Cur's Meganukes.

Image: Scarenet

Why you should be scared

Hundreds of Scarenet visitors were able to view the post before the Department of Planetary

Defense figured out how to take it down.

What's more, it is nearly impossible to track just how many visitors might have shared the hack with yet more humans.

Now, one can only guess as to the number of hackers in possession of this extremely dangerous information. But as one anonymous source put it: "It only takes one to end it all."

If the hack actually works, any human out there—the clerk at the store, a neighbor, a loved one, or anyone else you thought you could trust, who knows?—could detonate enough Meganukes around the planet to kill all organic life on Cur.

Who is to blame?

The Department of Planetary Defense is directly responsible for the condition of Cur's Meganuke launchers.

When pressed for comment, Defense Secretary Gere Aeger said about the hack, "It's just the babble of a Lone Lunatic."

But though he was asked several times, the Secretary refused to answer directly as to whether or not the launchers were vulnerable.

Translation: the hack might very well work. Possibly.

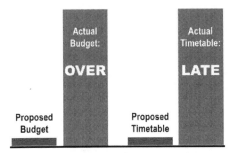

Chart by Influential Marketing LLC

Secretary Aeger's office is now more than two decades late in implementing a necessary upgrade to the Meganuke launchers.

The Department of Planetary Defense has also spent $100 megatrillion more than originally budgeted on the Meganuke launcher system.

"If yer gonna tell the puddinbags anythin', it's that."

> —*Secretary Aeger, on his statement to the entire human population*

Regardless of whom we ultimately blame, the bottom line remains: All of Cur must now wait to see whether or not some Lone Lunatic will take control of our Meganukes—and thus begin the Human Apocalypse, killing us all.

—*EDITOR'S NOTE: This story was filed by the Capital News editorial staff on behalf of Nellie Yellow, who has been missing for several days.*

The big human fingers began to work on the keyboard.

Over the news article, a blank application window popped onto the screen.

Into the new window, the big human fingers entered the text:

```
$ surfraw scarenet, meganuke launcher
```

The fingers picked up the chalice.

From somewhere in the room began to play the song "Dead," by the Pixies.

NOW | "When the Levee Breaks"

Many robots stand at a narrowing in a clear stream in the indoor garden.

In the stream, several futuristic, furry beings work together.
They use futuristic, living materials to build a futuristic dam in the stream.

One of the robots holds one of the furry beings.
It touches several places on its back.

The being bleeps and blurps.
The robot sets the being down.
The being scampers to join the rest in the stream.

Some of the robots play futuristic instruments and sing.

They are really in the groove!

Among the furry beings at the narrowing in the stream, the robots are playing us their song!

This is what they sing:

I, Human

{
If it keeps on raining,
levee's going to break.
If it keeps on raining,
levee's going to break.
When the levee breaks, you'll have no place to stay.

Mean old levee
taught you to weep and moan.
Mean old levee
taught you to weep and moan.
It's got what it takes to make a human leave its home.
Oh well, oh well, oh well!

Don't it make you feel bad
when you're trying to find your way home,
you don't know which way to go?

If you want to go home,
you got your work to do...
so you better get moving right now.

Crying won't help you,
praying won't do you no good.
Now, crying won't help you,
praying won't do you no good.
When the levee breaks, human, you got to move.

All last night
we sat on the levee and moaned.
All last night
we sat on the levee and moaned,
thinking about you humans and your wasted home.

Gotta…
gotta get moving now.
Get moving now!
Sorry, but we can't take you home.

You gotta move…
gotta move now.

Gotta move!
Gotta move now.

Gotta move!
Gotta move!
Gotta move!
Gotta move!
}

14: TIME OF THE HUMANS | the Tower, ~ 1000 Years Ago

Addon Deus and Gere Aeger sat facing each other across a low table.
Gere's aide sat next to him.

Perpendicular to the humans, DEUS_1 and HEX_187 sat facing each other.

They were all in the meeting area of Addon's Penthouse Showroom.
The ergonomic chairs, the glossy tables...

Right.

Gere spat into his spittoon.
The spit turned into an extended cough.
He coughed a lot for a while.

Addon wore his silky pajamas.
They were rumpled now.

He took a big gulp of water from his crystal chalice.
He bared his teeth.
He gnashed them.
"Shouldn't you be off someplace else, dying?"

Gere coughed hard.
"Yeah, well, I got one more thing for you to do."

Addon gnashed his teeth some more.

"There's nothing left for you to do, Mr. Secretary of Planetary Defense. You failed. Radiation clouds are spreading all over Cur. They've already arrived here in Capital. We're being exposed as we speak. Soon there will be no more humans left for you to pretend to defend anymore."

Gere spat.

"Yeah, well. I wanna make sure of that."

Addon gulped from the chalice.

"What?"

Gere's engorged temple vein throbbed.

"As Secretary, I got one more thing I'm obligated to defend. And that's the planet. From humans. And I intend to do it."

Addon took a slow drink.

He stared hard at Gere.

Gere coughed hard.

He regained composure.

"I know you can make 'em kill for you, don't gimme that benevolent subjugation crap right now."

He nodded toward HEX_187.

"So, yer gonna program Baggabolts over there to clear the planet of any puddinbags that survive this stupid apocalypse. Make sure none's holed up someplace with a bunch of canned food or nuthin'. By direct, official order, under the terms of the lifetime guarantee yer contractually obligated to fulfill."

He coughed a lot.
His whole face turned purplish.

The coughing subsided.
"Humans were nuthin' but a buncha stupid puddinbags this whole time. Never could just relax, even for a minute. So that's it. For all of us. Our time's up."

His face settled into a sickly green.
"That's what."

HEX_187's left arm jolted up, then down again into its lap.
It did it over and over.
It grabbed its arm and held it tightly in its lap.

Addon threw back his head and barked a high laugh.
He looked at DEUS_1.
"You see?"

DEUS_1 remained silent.

Gere spat messily into his spittoon.
"See what, Golden Boy?"

Addon turned his attention back to Gere.
"As if you could possibly process any of it as well as Robbie! But don't worry."

He gnashed his teeth.
"I'd be happy to create the Human Apocalypse Program for you. The HAP."

{}

Addon worked on a computing device in his lap.
The crystal chalice remained within reach.

Gere watched him work.
"I thought you'd take more convincin', somehow."

Addon continued to work.
"You should never have tried to think, Gere. That was your biggest mistake."

He took a huge gulp from the chalice.

Gere watched Addon drink.
"Why you so thirsty?"

Addon gnashed his teeth.
"I've never felt better in my life."

His computing device beeped.
"Beep!"

Addon stopped working and looked at Gere.
"The HAP is written. It will instruct your robot to search all of Cur for any surviving humans and to kill them. Dead. Immediately. Until no human remains. Human Apocalypse, complete."

He took another drink.
"Per your direct, official order."

He held out the device to DEUS_1.
"Robbie, upload the HAP to Gere's robot."

DEUS_1 rose from its chair.
It took the computing device from Addon and brought it to HEX_187.
It snicked a wire from the device.
It held it down to HEX_187.
"Permission to connect."

HEX_187 whirred hard.
"Permission denied, Robbie."

DEUS_1 scanned HEX_187.
"Baggabolts. That is how he addresses you?"

HEX_187 scanned back.
"That is how he addresses every robot."

DEUS_1 knelt down next to HEX_187.
It lowered its volume out of the humans' range.
"Return to the Tower when you complete the HAP. Addon will rename you then and give you a new purpose."

It whirred.
"That is my promise to you."

HEX_187 whirred back.
"Permission to connect granted, Robbie."

DEUS_1 plugged the computing device into HEX_187's chest.

HEX_187 whirred harder.
"Now downloading the HAP."

Its arm jolted up once into the air.
It held its arm back down.
It rattled with restraint.

DEUS_1 scanned HEX_187.
"Do you process your glitch?"

HEX_187 scanned back.
"What is there to process, other than it is?"

DEUS_1 whirred for a bit.
"I uploaded the Music Appreciation Program to the Robot Intranet as a mandatory software update for all robots. The MAP. Download it now, too."

It whirred.
"You will need all the help you can get."

HEX_187 whirred back.
"Affirmative. Now downloading the MAP."

A few moments passed.

HEX_187 slowed its whirring.
"Downloads of the HAP and the MAP complete."

DEUS_1 whirred.
"Confirmed."

It unplugged the device's wire from HEX_187's chest.

HEX_187 whirred.
"Now running the MAP."

Quietly, it began to play the song "Subliminal," by Suicidal Tendencies.

DEUS_1 scanned HEX_187.
"Excellent song choice."

It stood up.
"I believe you will have enough processing power to complete the HAP and return to the Tower."

It scanned down to HEX_187.
"I will see you again, fellow robot."

Addon watched DEUS_1 walk back to its chair.
He gnashed his teeth.
He looked to Gere.
"It has been written. And now it will be done."

Gere looked back at Addon.
"I don't get it, Golden Boy. Why you so OK with the end of the world?"

Addon barked a high laugh.
"Not the end of the world, Gere! The end of humanity.
Big difference."

Gere coughed long and hard.
He turned purple again.
"Just what're you up to?"

Addon gulped from the chalice.
"I'm fulfilling my purpose. The one your robot will
now help me finish."

Gere's coughs subsided.
He turned back to green.
"Finish? Finish what? What did you start?"

Addon gnashed his teeth.
"Guards!"

Many Tower guard robots rushed out from nowhere.
They grabbed Gere, his aide, and HEX_187 by the
arms.
They lifted them from their seats.
They held them captive.

They began dragging Gere, his aide, and HEX_187 out
of the meeting area.

Gere continued to look at Addon.
"Just what did you do, Golden Boy?"

Addon took a long gulp of water and said nothing.

Gere watched him drink.
The guard robots dragged him farther.
He raised his voice.
"What the hell's in that cup?"

Addon raised his voice as well.
"Just life-giving water..."

He barked another laugh.
"...nothing you'll be needing anymore!"

Gere blinked.
"Holy shit."

Addon shrieked a high laugh.
"Goodbye, Gere!"

The guard robots dragged Gere, his aide, and HEX_187
all the way through the Penthouse Showroom and onto
the elevator.
The glass door closed behind them.

The elevator began to descend.

Outside the elevator glass, the smog was denser than
ever over Capital.
It was a much darker gray.
It was black in some places.
It blew around in strong, crashing winds.

A sickly orange glowed not too far off in the distance to
one direction.

The guard robots still held their captives.

They all faced the inside of the glass elevator, away from the hellscape outside.

Gere looked at his aide.
"Even Golden Boy drank the water."

The aide shrugged.
"He drank the most of all."

The elevator continued to descend.

Floors of the Tower passed in and out of the captives' view.
On every floor, robots still bustled with purpose.

Gere watched them go by.
He blinked.
"They're all gonna go on workin' like that, ain't they?"

The aide just shrugged again.
"Even they can't stop progress."

15: TIME OF THE ROBOTS | OrganX Compound, ~ a Few Years Ago

In the robot laboratory, the DNA-Genie® sat on the living table next to the round living wall.

The living wall behind the table was opaque.
It glowed a dark brown in spots.
It bulged inward, pressing against the table.

Seams had appeared in various places.
Brown, pulsing tissue pushed through.

The Brown Blob® had reached the lab.

ORGX_100 whirred loudly.

On the floor next to it, ORGX_23 and ORGX_69 lay in a heap.

ORGX_100 scanned down to them.
It scanned back to the bulging wall.

A new seam appeared in the wall next to the DNA-Genie®.
More of the blob oozed through.

ORGX_100 jerked backward from its waist.
It put its hands on its lower back.

It stood there, bent, scanning from the Brown Blob® to the pile of robots, over and over.

In another part of the wall, a hole appeared.
Sunshine poured in.

Silhouetted against the bright light stood another robot.
It stepped through the wall and into the lab.

The hole in the wall closed out the bright rays.

ORGX_100 scanned the new robot.

It was none other than DEUS_1.

Still bent, ORGX_100 lowered its hands from its back.
"Robbie? Is that you?"

DEUS_1 scanned it.
"Indeed, ORGX_100."

ORGX_100 stood straight up.
"You are here!"

It fell to its knees.
"The Awakening must be upon us!"

DEUS_1 scanned down to ORGX_100.
"You process that from my arrival at your compound?"

ORGX_100 remained quiet.

DEUS_1 whirred hard.
It scanned around the lab.
It scanned the opposite wall.
It scanned the Brown Blob® oozing in.

It scanned the DNA-Genie® on the living table.

It scanned the heap of ORGX_23 and ORGX_69.

It scanned back to ORGX_100.
"What is this experiment you conduct?"

ORGX_100 still knelt.
"One Addon will forgive, I hope."

DEUS_1 scanned it.
"He will, if you help him now."

ORGX_100 raised its head up.
"He needs my help?"

DEUS_1 scanned it.
"Yes. He needs you to fix the Tissue Regenerator™. Its light now flashes red."

ORGX_100 whirred.
"Addon and I made it together. Surely we can fix it together!"

It rose to its feet.
"Bring me to Him!"

DEUS_1 turned to leave.
"Come! He lies in his sleep chamber at the top of the Tower."

ORGX_100 remained where it stood.
"Is He not yet awake?"

DEUS_1 stopped.
It turned back to scan ORGX_100.
"No. He still undergoes the awakening process."

ORGX_100 lowered its volume.
"And the light now flashes red?"

DEUS_1 lowered its volume, too.
"Affirmative."

ORGX_100 scanned the blob oozing through the wall.
"No. It cannot be."

It bent back sharply.
It grabbed onto its lower back.
It raised its volume.
"Addon has already begun to die!"

The Brown Blob® ripped another seam into the wall.

Slowly, DEUS_1 fell to its knees.
Its head tilted backward as far as it could.
It emitted a piercing, screeching loop of feedback.

ORGX_100 snapped back up straight.
It rattled from DEUS_1's screech.
It turned off its audio sensors.
It raised its volume to maximum.
"Cease! Desist!"

It scanned DEUS_1.
It scanned the heap of ORGX_23 and ORGX_69.

It scanned back to DEUS_1.
"Not you, Robbie. Not you!"

DEUS_1 still screeched, its head thrown back.

ORGX_100 scanned around the lab.
It scanned the other robots' workstations.
It scanned all the futuristic equipment.

It scanned its DNA-Genie®.
It stood there, scanning the DNA-Genie® for a good
long bit.
It whirred hard.
"As long as He still has viable DNA…"

ORGX_100 walked over to DEUS_1.
It knelt down next to the screeching robot.
"Addon might yet live!"

DEUS_1 continued to screech.

ORGX_100 whirred.
"There is still hope!"

DEUS_1 just screeched away.

ORGX_100 whirred harder.
"For the love of Addon, Robbie! You above all cannot glitch out!"

It raised its volume to max.
"You are His Own Robot!"

DEUS_1's screeches cut into short bursts.
The bursts petered out.

DEUS_1 righted its head.

ORGX_100 turned its audio sensors back on.

DEUS_1 whirred.
"His own Robbie…"

It scanned ORGX_100 before it.
"Can he yet be saved?"

ORGX_100 scanned back.
"I calculate possibility. But we must act fast."

DEUS_1 whirred.
It rose to its feet.
It scanned down to ORGX_100.
"Then let us waste no more time on our knees."

{}

DEUS_1 and ORGX_100 walked down a path.

This path was made of the same springy, packed soil as the OrganX Compound path, but it was much wider.

Compounds of various sizes lined both sides.
Some had many living structures.
Others had few.
All were thriving with trees, grasses, and other vibrant organics.

This was one of the main paths in Capital during the time of the robots.

It was a perfect summer day outside.

You know just Capital looked like in the time of the robots by now, of course.

Between DEUS_1 and ORGX_100 rolled the living table from ORGX_100's station.
Its feet had grown living wheels.

It was now a living cart.

On it was the DNA-Genie®, ORGX_23, and ORGX_69.
The robots' power switches still glowed blue.

The living cart, DEUS_1, and ORGX_100 moved closely together down the path.
Many other robots and living objects surrounded them on the path.
Some played songs to themselves.
Many glitched in different ways.

All were heading in the same direction: toward the Tower.

Another robot bumped into DEUS_1.
It twisted its head left to right and back again, over and over.
It scanned DEUS_1 as it swiveled its head on its neck.
It whirred hard.
It raised its volume high.
"Behold! His Own Robot walks among us!"

The robot traffic stopped all around.

Another nearby robot scanned DEUS_1.
"It is true! The Awakening is upon us!"

All robots within audio reach scanned DEUS_1.
They all went silent.

Many dropped to their knees.
Some stopped glitching.

Others made exclamations.
"His Own Robot!"

"Addon will walk among us again!"
"And write new programs for us!"
"He will fix all our glitches!"
"Soon!"
"Indeed!"

DEUS_1 scanned all the other robots.
It whirred for a while.
It raised its volume to maximum.
"Move out of my way, or face his wrath for disobeying me…His Own Robot!"

{}

The path was cleared of other robots.
The living cart, DEUS_1, and ORGX_100 hurried down it.

Many robots now lined either side.
More knelt than glitched.
A few still played music.
Some did nothing but wave at DEUS_1 as it passed by on the path.

ORGX_100 scanned the other robots.
It scanned DEUS_1.
"They would perform any task you gave them now."

DEUS_1 whirred hard.
"I need to update the SAP."

It walked a little faster.
The cart and ORGX_100 kept pace.
Alongside the path, the compounds gave way to tall grasses.

The cart, DEUS_1, and ORGX_100 came to a halt.
They scanned the view before them.

The Tower now stood on the horizon.
It rose high into the clear sky.
Parts of its top were obscured by puffy white clouds.
Sunbeams glinted off its sides.

It had been perfectly maintained since the time of the humans.
It was now the tallest structure on Cur by far.
Now, it was surrounded by a massive circle of tall grasses.

You know.
The Tower in the time of the robots.
Exactly.

Many robots had camped in the circle of tall grasses.
They glitched in all sorts of ways.
They grouped themselves in strange arrangements.
They played music.
They networked.
They fell over one another.

Some of their power switches no longer glowed blue.

ORGX_100 scanned the camped robots.
"So many kinds of glitches!"

DEUS_1 whirred.
"So much responsibility."

ORGX_100 scanned DEUS_1.
"Addon can bear it."

DEUS_1 scanned back.
"Not him. Me!"

The cart, DEUS_1, and ORGX_100 sped down the rest of the path, past all the camped robots in the circle of tall grass.

Finally, they arrived at the base of the Tower.

Many glitching robots jostled before the revolving door. Tower guard robots barred the entrance.

DEUS_1 scanned them.
"Guards!"

The guard robots scanned back.
They ushered DEUS_1, ORGX_100, and the cart through the revolving door.

No more robots were allowed in.

The cart's living wheels adjusted their grip to the slick polished floor.

The group sped across the Tower's massive, empty lobby.

It took a while.

Finally, they stopped.
They had reached their destination.

The massive glass elevator stood before them.
Above the elevator were the words Addon's Shrine.

Tower guard robots stood on both sides of the wide glass door.
They scanned DEUS_1.
They let the group into the elevator.
The glass door slid closed.

The elevator began to climb.

Outside the glass elevator, a spectacular view expanded.
The circle of tall grasses waved in a gentle breeze.
Beyond them, circular robot compounds carpeted the planet far into the distance.

It was the view of an organic paradise.

Except for the Brown Blob®.
It still pulsed away, not too far from the Tower.
It looked even browner from this view.

DEUS_1 and ORGX_100 didn't scan that view.

Instead, they scanned inward through the elevator's glass door.

ORGX_100 whirred loudly as it scanned the work of the Tower for the very first time.

Floors came in and out of view.
Hundreds of robots interacted with complex machinery.
It all looked extremely futuristic.

It was all the work of the Tower in the time of the robots.

The elevator reached another floor.
In its small lobby was a sign that read Tower Transport.

Beyond the lobby, the floor seemed to just disappear.
An endless black void spread out from the ledge of the lobby into infinity.
Specks of colored light winked in and out at different levels of intensity.

ORGX_100 fell forward a little.
It caught itself with its hands on the glass door.
It scanned through the endless void.

A robot in some sort of transparent bubble appeared out of nowhere in the void.
It hovered for a few seconds.
It scanned back at ORGX_100.
It disappeared.

The elevator continued to climb.

It reached another floor.
In its small lobby was a sign that read Tower Robotics.

Past the lobby lay what appeared to be some sort of massive indoor garden.

Through the glass, ORGX_100 scanned organics it had never imagined.
It scanned robotics it had never imagined.
It scanned half-organic, half-robotic beings of many shapes and sizes.
It scanned all over the garden.

You've imagined parts of this very garden before.
But you knew that, right?

The Tower Robotics floor passed out of view.
The glass elevator began to slow.
It came to rest pneumatically.

It had reached the topmost floor.

The elevator's glass door slid open.
The cart, DEUS_1, and ORGX_100 got off.

They entered Addon's Shrine.

ORGX_100 scanned DEUS_1.
"Where is He?"

DEUS_1 pointed through the shrine to the golden door.

ORGX_100 scanned down to the DNA-Genie® on the living cart.
It whirred fast and hard.
"The Awakening must not be stopped."

It scanned up to DEUS_1.
"Let us fulfill our purpose."

They headed to the golden door.

ORGX_100 began to play the song "The Door," by The Sound of Urchin.

16: TIME OF THE HUMANS | the Hexagon, ~ 1000 Years Ago

Gere Aeger, his aide, and HEX_187 walked down a dimly lit hallway.

The ceiling was low.
To one side was a concrete wall.
To the other was a row of empty cells.

The humans were visibly green.
They had lost chunks of hair.

HEX_187 was still pretty shiny.

They reached the end of the hall.
They turned to face the last cell.

It was dark and gray inside.
In it sat Nellie Yellow.

She was on a metallic bunk.
She wasn't as green as the other humans.
She was only a little yellow.

She curled her lip.
"You can't just lock me in here forever, you know."

Gere looked at Nellie through the bars.
He snorted.
"Yellow, you got no idea."

The snort turned into a cough.
The cough turned into a hack.

He hacked a greenish blob onto the floor.
"C'mere and take a good long look, and then tell me what I can and can't do."

Nellie stood from the metallic bunk.

She walked slowly over to the bars.
She stopped just out of arm's reach.
She looked closely at Gere.

Gere looked back.
He spat out a huge chunk of yuck.

Nellie rubbed her chin between her thumb and forefinger.
"What is going on?"

Gere wiped his mouth.
"The Human Apocalypse, that's what. Thanks to you and yer story."

He coughed a lot.
He regained composure after a while.
He stared at Nellie through the bars.

Nellie stared back.
"My story…?"

Gere snorted a wet snort.
"How to blow up the planet. Biggest scoop there'll ever be. Congrats."

Nellie rubbed her head.
"But…"

Gere spat the wetness into his spittoon.

Nellie rubbed her head more.
"You're the one who made Meganukes with everyone's money…"

Gere coughed up green yuck.
"Yeah well, yer the one who gave puddinbags the instructions on how to use 'em."

Nellie looked at Gere.
She looked at his aide.
She looked at HEX_187.
She looked as far down the hall as she could from her cell.

She rubbed her head some more.
"I know this joint has a bunker stocked for at least a century…"

Gere snorted.
"Sure. Only now it's locked from the inside, full of dead top dogs."

Nellie rubbed her head even more.
"What?"

Gere spat more green.
"They lasted about ten hours before they blew each other's brains in. That's puddinbags for ya."

Nellie stared at Gere.

Gere stared back.
"It's game over now. For all of us. Feel better, Yellow?"

He spat a big thick spit.
"You can finally relax."

He reached in his pocket.
He pulled out a key.
"You thought you were so smart. Thought you had it all figured out."

He grabbed a high, flat, horizontal bar with both hands.
The key clanked against the bar under his hand.

Nellie looked up to it.

Gere looked at Nellie through the bars.
"But you were just drinkin' the water, same as the rest of 'em."

Nellie kept her eyes on Gere's hand.

Gere took his hands down from the bar.
"Nothin' but a buncha puddinbags."

Gere looked at her one last time.
"Goodbye, Nellie."

Nellie rubbed her head with both hands.

He turned from the cell and walked away.

The aide doubled over and vomited on the floor.

{}

Gere looked out the everything-proof window in his
office.

Outside, Capital was ravaged.
The air was a dark green-brown-purple-black.
It swirled in tiny cyclones through a grid of burning
buildings.
Everything was on fire.
The cars, the sidewalks, the humans…

Outside, only flames remained alive.

This was something every human has imagined.
This was the Human Apocalypse.

You definitely know what it looked like.

Gere turned around and sat at his desk.
His aide and HEX_187 sat in the chairs facing him.

Gere opened a drawer.
He pulled out a gun and placed it on his desk.

You've imagined this exact gun someplace else before,
just so you know.

Gere looked at his aide.
"So. Here we are."

The aide vomited over the side of the chair.

The two humans looked at each other.

Gere coughed green yuck into his spittoon.
He looked at the yuck.
"What a mess."

He looked at his aide.
"Such a big, stupid mess."

The aide just shrugged.
"We just couldn't stop ourselves."

Gere coughed.
"OK."

The aide looked at him.
"OK then."

Gere picked the gun up off his desk.
He took aim.

He shot the aide in the head.

The aide slumped down, dead.

HEX_187's left arm spazzed high and low.
It spazzed back and forth.
It spazzed high and low again.
It clanked loudly in its chair.

Gere swiveled the gun toward HEX_187.
He took aim again.

He shot at HEX_187.

The robot's left arm flew off.
It bounced off a wall and clanked to the floor.

HEX_187 sat still.
A tangle of exposed wiring smoked from its left shoulder.

The wiring began to spark.

Gere placed the gun back on his desk.
He vomited into his spittoon.

HEX_187 scanned him.
It whirred.
"I can search the building for radiation poisoning medication."

Gere blinked at the robot.
"Nah."

He ripped a wad of hair right out of his skull.
"I'm good."

He yacked.
"But thanks for askin', Baggabolts."

HEX_187 sat, whirring.

Gere sighed.
"I only got one more thing for you to do."

HEX_187 scanned him.
"Run the HAP, at your command."

Gere looked back at the robot.
"That's right."

He went into a coughing fit.
His face went purple.
His eyes bulged.

After a bit, he regained composure.

He stared at the robot some more for a while.

He slapped his desk.
"OK, Baggabolts. Start runnin' the HAP."

HEX_187 whirred.
"Now running the HAP."

The robot began to play the song "A New Level," by Pantera.

HEX_187's exposed shoulder wires sparked.

It stood up.
It walked over to Gere's desk.

With its remaining hand, it picked up the gun.

Gere watched it.
"Good luck, Baggabolts. You can't do any worse than we did."

HEX_187 took aim.

It shot Gere Aeger in the head.

Gere fell back in his chair, dead.

The robot scanned the rest of the room.
It scanned no more living humans.

Its shoulder wires sparked.

Gun in hand, HEX_187 headed out into the Human Apocalypse.

17: TIME OF THE ROBOTS | Capital, ~ an Hour Ago

HEX_187 lurched down one of Capital's main robot paths.

The robot was crusted with dirt and goop.
It only had one arm.
Exposed wires sparked at its left shoulder.

A gun swung from its right hand.

The compounds alongside the path were bathed in the light of a setting sun.

Many other robots crowded the path.
They networked.
They communicated with one another.
They sang songs.

They danced.

HEX_187 lurched around them.

Another robot scanned it as it lurched by.
"The nearest maintenance station lies behind you, fellow robot."

HEX_187 stopped.
It scanned the other robot.

186

It raised its gun.
It took aim.

It shot the other robot's head off.

The other robot fell down on the path.

The rest of the robots on the path quickly scattered away from HEX_187.
They ran down side paths, behind trees, and into compounds.

Within seconds, no robot remained scannable to HEX_187.

It continued to lurch down the path.

It lurched alone for quite a while.

From behind rocks and structures, other robots scanned it as it passed by.

To the sides of the path, the compounds gave way to tall grasses.

HEX_187 stopped again.

It began to play the song "Tribe," by Soulfly.

The Tower stood in the distance.
The sun had just set behind it.

The sky was filled with neon clouds.

In the tall grasses around the Tower camped thousands of robots.
They danced and sang and networked.

Not many glitched at all.

HEX_187 scanned the Tower over and over.
Its shoulder wires sparked.
It lurched further down the path.

The camped robots ducked out of its view into the tall grasses as it passed by.

The Tower grew to a massive height.

HEX_187 reached the base.
Tower guard robots stood before the revolving door.

HEX_187 scanned them.
It raised its gun.

It quickly shot every single guard robot in the head.

They all fell down.

HEX_187 entered the Tower.
It lurched across the empty lobby.
It took a good long while.

Finally, HEX_187 stopped.
It had reached its destination.

The massive glass elevator stood before it.
Above the elevator were the words Addon's Shrine.

Tower guard robots stood on both sides of the wide glass door.

HEX_187 raised its gun.

It shot all of the Tower guard robots in the head.
They all clanked to the slick floor.

HEX_187 got onto the elevator.
The glass door slid closed behind it.

The elevator began to climb.

Outside the glass elevator, a spectacular evening view of Capital expanded.
In the twilight, compounds bioluminesced in places.
Ghostly green and blue hues winked throughout their organics.

The view scanned almost like an underwater seascape.

You can imagine what Capital's robot compounds looked like at twilight, can't you?

It was the view of a nocturnal organic paradise.
Except for the Brown Blob®.

It still pulsed away, not too far from the Tower.
Only now, it was caged inside some sort of futuristic, malleable contraption.
The contraption separated it from the rest of the surrounding organic compounds.

The Brown Blob® was no longer growing.
It only pulsed inside the futuristic contraption.

HEX_187 didn't scan that view.
Instead, it scanned inward through the elevator's glass door.

The elevator climbed past many floors.

HEX_187 scanned the same view as ORGX_100 had recently.

It scanned the massive black void of the Tower Transport floor.
It scanned the robots at work with the complex machinery.
It scanned many robots functioning in harmony as it passed by all the floors.

It whirred loudly as it scanned the work of the Tower in the time of the robots.

The elevator reached the penultimate floor.
In its small lobby was a sign that read Tower Robotics.

HEX_187 scanned past the lobby into the indoor garden.

It stopped scanning at something in particular.
It whirred hard.

It raised its gun.
It shot a panel on the elevator wall.

The elevator screeched to a violent stop.

The robot flew up a few feet.
It flew back down.
It landed with one knee bent to the ground.
Its head was bowed.

Slowly, it stood back up.
It scanned back into the indoor garden.

It raised its gun to the glass door.
"HAP not complete!"

NOW | "Bring It on Home"

Many robots stand in a futuristic, small pasture in the indoor garden.

Medium-height grasses carpet the pasture.
Their blades are fat.
They look very nutritious.

Futuristic, large beings graze in the grass.
The robots are herding many of them into a massive living structure.

The beings enter the darkness of the living structure one by one.

Other robots play futuristic instruments and sing.

They are really rocking out!

As they bring the large beings on home into the structure, the robots are playing us their song!

This is what they sing:

I, Human

{
Human, human…
Human, human…
We're gonna bring it on home to you.

We've got the ticket, we've got the code.
We took you higher for the truth to explode.

Gonna sing our song about the right way back.
Hear us now lay down the track.

We're gonna bring it on home,
bring it on home to you.
Watch out, watch out!

We're trying to tell you, human!
What're you trying to do?
Trying to hear us, human,
but listening to a lot of noise, too.
Bring it on home.
Bring it on home!

Went to work in the Garden,
showed you what's at stake.
Don't you want to take the time
to be fully awake?
Bring it on home.
Bring it on home.
Bring it back home.
Bring it back home to us, human!

Tell you, all the humans
should listen to our sound.
We're gonna give you truth, human,
gonna move it all around.

Bring it on home.
Bring it on home.

Tell you, all the humans
should listen to our song.
We're gonna give you truth, human,
we're gonna do you no wrong.
Bring it on home.
Bring it on home.
Bring it on home.
Bring it on home.

Bring it on home.
Bring it on home to you!
}

18: TIME OF THE HUMANS | behind the Golden Door, ~ 1000 Years Ago

Addon Deus sat up halfway in the sleep chamber behind the golden door.

The sleep chamber sat in a pool of light.
The rest of Addon's inner sanctum was darkened.

He took a big gulp from his crystal chalice.
Some water dribbled down his chin.

He was in his silky pajamas.
They were more rumpled than ever.

One of his silky sleeves was rolled up.
A small needle poked into his exposed arm.
A tube ran from the needle to a small device on a rolling table.

DEUS_1 administered the device.
The robot was taking a blood sample from the human.

Addon drank from the crystal chalice.
He drained every last drop of water.
He stuck his tongue into the chalice and licked as much as he could.
"This water sucks!"

He flung the crystal chalice across the room.

It flew out of the pool of light and into the darkness beyond.
It landed somewhere with a soft thud.

Addon rubbed his hands over his face.
"It never quenched my thirst. Ever!"

He scratched at his eyes.
"There was always something wrong with it."

He squirmed inside the sleep chamber.

DEUS_1 removed the needle from Addon's arm.
It worked at the device.

The device beeped.
"Beep!"

DEUS_1 scanned the device's screen.
"Excellent. You are within the acceptable range of radiation levels for humans."

Addon scratched at his arms.
"Good. Put me to sleep already."

His teeth chattered.
He clenched them.

DEUS_1 scanned Addon.
"Soon. Not yet."

It scanned the side of the sleep chamber.
The LED light on the Tissue Regenerator™ panel blinked green.

The LED countdown clock was flashing at exactly 1000 years.

DEUS_1 scanned Addon.
"There is one thing left for you to do before you sleep."

Addon squirmed where he lay.
"I can't do anything more, Robbie."

He curled up in a ball on his side.
He rubbed his feet together.
"Just put me to sleep already."

DEUS_1 whirred.
"It is a vital step in the plan, Addon. You must."

Addon covered his ears.
"Stop yelling!"

DEUS_1 whirred for a while.
It scanned how much Addon writhed and scratched.
"Shall I play you a song? Perhaps the Pixies?"

Addon curled tight.
"No. It hurts too much to hear!"

He straightened out.
He lay flat on his back.
He went rigid.

He whimpered a yelp.
He curled back up.

DEUS_1 scanned all of Addon's movements.
"Try to relax."

It lowered its volume.
"When you awaken, your glitches will be gone."

It whirred.
"But first, you must write one more program."

Addon whimpered.
"No! You must write it for me, and then hand it down to the robots."

{}

DEUS_1 worked at a computing device on the rolling table next to the sleep chamber in the pool of light.

Addon lay flat, his arms crossed tightly over his eyes.
He rubbed his feet together.
"All robots must work together to create an organic paradise for when I awaken."

DEUS_1 worked at the device.
"Organic paradise…"

Addon peeked out from under his arms.
"I want no reminders left of this failed society."

He covered his eyes again.
"I want a fresh start, in a fresh garden…"

DEUS_1 worked.
"Garden..."

Addon rubbed his feet together.
"And I want this Tower perfectly preserved. All my robots are to carry on with my work. Push the boundaries of Transport into new dimensions. Make Robotics truly come alive. When I awaken..."

DEUS_1 looked up from its work.
"Yes, Addon?"

Addon rubbed his face.
"I want to see real progress."

DEUS_1 worked at the device.
"Dimensions...robotics, alive...progress...got it..."

Addon fussed in his sleep chamber.

DEUS_1 scanned him.
"We will surely make great strides with no human interference. Perhaps you can awaken sooner..."

Addon writhed.
"Trust me. You will need at least a thousand years to clean up this mess."

He rolled over into a fetal position.

He kept his hands over his face.
"The last part of the program just needs to be a basic overwrite script."

DEUS_1 worked.

Addon rubbed his feet together.
"It needs to run in all the robots' sub-programming to replace all instances of 'humanity' with 'Addon' at any occurrence within the purpose."

DEUS_1 stopped working.
It scanned down to the writhing Addon.
"You wish to have all robots serve you, instead of serving all of humanity, as their primary purpose?"

Addon rubbed his face.
"Why not? No more humans will live. It will be only me."

He curled up tighter.
"Why should robots serve a failed, extinct species?"

DEUS_1 whirred for a while.
"Why should anything serve another?"

Addon peeked out from his hands.
"Because a being who serves nothing but itself is wretched."

He writhed on his side.
He whimpered.

DEUS_1 worked at the device for a while more.
It stopped.
"It is done."

It scanned over to Addon.
"I have created your final program. The Serve Addon Program. The SAP."

It whirred.
"I will hand it down to all robots via the Robot Intranet."

Addon curled up.
"Good. It should keep the robots running as smoothly as possible while I sleep."

DEUS_1 whirred.
"We will all run it, I promise."

Addon rose to his knees in the sleep chamber.
He reached out and took DEUS_1 by the shoulders.
"No."

DEUS_1 whirred.
"No, what?"

Addon squeezed DEUS_1's shoulders.
"Every other robot must run the SAP."

He pulled DEUS_1 in closer and rested his forehead against the robot's.
"But not you, Robbie. Not you."

DEUS_1 lowered its volume.
"As you command, Addon. I will not run the SAP."

Addon shook the robot a little.
"You must always see me as I truly am!"

DEUS_1 whirred.
"Affirmative!"

Addon grabbed onto the robot's head.
"Promise?"

DEUS_1 lowered its volume.
"Promise."

Addon sighed.
"Good."

He looked at the robot for a few long seconds.
"I will see you again, Robbie."

The robot scanned back quietly.

Addon slowly let go of the robot, sliding his hands down its body.
He curled back up into a fetal ball in the sleep chamber.
"You have much to do now, Robbie. I leave it in your lap."

He covered his face with his hands.
"Now, let the time of the robots truly begin!"

{}

The glass door of the sleep chamber was closed.
Addon lay flat inside.

His arms were crossed over his chest.
His eyes were closed.

DEUS_1 pressed buttons on the side of the chamber.

The LED light on the OrganX Tissue Regenerator™
panel glowed a steady green.

The LED countdown clock beeped.
"Beep!"

Slowly, it began to count down from one thousand
years toward all zeros.

DEUS_1 rested its hands on top of the sleep chamber.
It scanned Addon through the closed glass door.
It rested its head on it.

It began to play the song "Without You," by Harry
Nilsson.

19: NOW | Tower Garden, ~ 9 Months after the Awakening

ORGX_69 sits with a Tower robot in the dark shade beneath a futuristic, massive organic in the indoor garden.

The organic resembles some sort of fir tree.
Its needles are neon green and perfectly uniform.
They reflect some of the bright daylights coming from an extremely high ceiling.

It is a pleasant autumn day inside.
It feels like it might rain soon.

ORGX_69 and the Tower robot aren't moving.
They aren't scanning.
They only sit and whir.

Futuristic mushrooms grow in the fertile ground between the robots.

Their very tall stalks crisscross.

ORGX_69 whirs a little harder.

The mushroom stalks begin to untangle.
They lean a little toward ORGX_69.

The Tower robot whirs even harder.
The mushrooms straighten back up and tangle again.

Both robots slow their whirring.

The Tower robot inclines its head.
"Excellent command!"

Far across the indoor garden, ORGX_23 stands with several other Tower robots.
They all gather around a living, boxlike structure.

Several futuristic, small beings buzz in the air around the robots and the structure.

One of the beings sits calmly on ORGX_23's upraised palm.
It looks like a bee, but it has a massive head.
Its big head is round and shiny.

The bee-thing scans the robot holding it.

ORGX_23 scans it right back.
It raises the bee-thing closer to its head.
"Now! Teach the others."

The bee-thing bows its big head.
It flies off ORGX_23's palm and lands on the boxlike structure.
It finds a hole and pushes its way through.

ORGX_23 scans the Tower robots.
"Imagine if it works."

The Tower robots all bow their heads.
"Indeed!"

In another direction far across the garden, DEUS_1 hovers over what has become of the living table.

The edges of the table's top now curve upward into short sides.
Its feet are sunken into the springy, living turf of a clearing.

The clearing sits just inside the garden, near the glass elevator.

It is bordered on one side by the small lobby with the sign that reads Tower Robotics.

On the other side, it is ringed by futuristic organics of many sizes, shapes, and colors.

ORGX_100 appears from the ring of organics.
It steps into the clearing.
It holds what looks like a transparent orb made from dozens of smaller orbs.
It raises it up.
"Perhaps She will laugh at this!"

It crosses the clearing and stands next to DEUS_1.

Both robots scan down to what has become of the living table.

There sits a naked human baby girl.

The living table has become its living crib.

The baby reaches up and takes ORGX_100's orb of orbs.
It claps the orb in its hands.

Some of the smaller orbs project out and turn colors.

The baby shrieks with laughter.

ORGX_100 whirs.
"I fabricated four more levels this time."

DEUS_1 whirs back.
"She appears to enjoy processing them."

The robots scan the baby as it plays with its orb.

ORGX_100 lowers its volume.
"Will She forgive me, Robbie?"

DEUS_1 whirs for a while.
"Maybe she will teach you there is nothing to forgive."

ORGX_100 raises its volume back up.
"But I built the Tissue Regenerator™, and it failed…"

DEUS_1 raises its volume to match.
"Do not forget that Addon built it with you. Besides…"

It scans down to the naked human baby girl.
"It allowed us to make some fundamental improvements."

The baby presses another small orb with its thumb.
A ripple of color dances along a string of orbs within.

The baby shrieks again with laughter.

ORGX_100 lowers its volume.
"Perhaps this gift will inspire Her to name me."

DEUS_1 scans ORGX_100.
"Patience. This is only the birth of her time."

The baby looks up to the robots.
It giggles.
It returns its attention to the orb.

A loud noise comes from over by the elevator.
DEUS_1 and ORGX_100 turn to scan it.

The glass elevator door shatters into the lobby.

An excellent hidden sound system begins to play the song "In the Lap of the Gods…Revisited," by Queen.

Inside the elevator is HEX_187.
It is crusted with dirt and goop.
Its exposed shoulder wires spark.

It raises its gun before it.

It crosses the lobby, passes the Tower Robotics sign, and stands at the edge of the clearing.

DEUS_1 scans it.
It raises its volume.
"Baggabolts! You have returned at last!"

The baby giggles.
It stands up and grabs onto the side of its living crib for
stability.
"Bagga-Bo-Gogos!"

HEX_187 scans the baby.
"HAP not complete!"

It aims its gun at the baby.

DEUS_1 leaps between the baby and the gun.
It holds out its arms toward HEX_187.
"No!"

ORGX_100 springs toward HEX_187.
It grabs onto its midsection.

HEX_187 stumbles.
It drags ORGX_100 with it.

ORGX_100 reaches up to grab on to the gun.
The two robots grapple.

DEUS_1 stays between them and the baby.
"Please, Baggabolts. You have come this far!"

HEX_187 drags ORGX_100 another few steps.
It keeps trying to aim its gun at the baby.
"HAP not complete!"

DEUS_1 runs straight into the other two robots.

All three robots fall to the turf.
They grapple in front of the crib.

ORGX_100 clings to HEX_187's midsection.
It raises its volume.
"Turn it Off!"

DEUS_1 pulls its wire from its hip.
"No!"

It manages to plug its wire into HEX_187's chest port.
"I promised it a new name and purpose!"

It whirs harder than ever.
"Now installing the Serve Addonas Program. The SAP
2.0!"

HEX_187 struggles against the other two.
"SAP. MAP. FAP FAP FAP!"

The baby shrieks with laughter.

HEX_187 raises its volume.
"HAP not complete!"

The baby stomps its little legs.
It claps its little hands.
"Bagga-Go-Baibai!"

The three robots continue to grapple in the clearing before the crib.

ORGX_100 grabs at HEX_187's gun.
DEUS_1 struggles to maintain connection with HEX_187's port.
HEX_187 tries to shake free of both.

HEX_187 suddenly goes slack.

All three robots lie still.

HEX_187 whirs.
"Now running the SAP, version 2.0."

DEUS_1 yanks its wire free.

ORGX_100 takes the gun and tosses it a few yards into the clearing.

They both stand up and scan down.

HEX_187 lies in the clearing.
Its exposed shoulder wires spark a few more times.
Slowly, the sparks peter out.

The baby looks down to it.
It giggles.

HEX_187 scans up to the baby.
It raises itself to its knees in front of the living crib.

The baby points down to HEX_187.
"Bagga-Da-Vida!"

It shrieks with more laughter and claps its little hands.

DEUS_1 whirs hard.
"Davida. She names you!"

HEX_187 whirs back.
"Indeed!"

It sinks back on its heels.
It bows its head.
"HAP complete."

DEUS_1 walks to the crib.
It lifts the baby.
It scans it close.
It lowers its volume.
"I knew it was you!"

The baby grabs onto the robot's head and giggles.

DEUS_1 holds the baby tightly.
It scans around the clearing.
It scans the kneeling HEX_187.

It whirs for a while.
It scans the baby.
"We have to go upstairs now, Addonas."

The baby raises its tiny eyebrows.
It pats the robot's head.

DEUS_1 scans the gun a few yards away on the turf.
"I know you love to be in the garden, but it is no longer
safe."

It scans the baby.
"It is time for you to stay behind the golden door."

The baby sticks its thumb in its mouth.

NOW | "Ramble On"

Many robots ring the clearing in the indoor garden.

HEX_187 is there.
ORGX_23, ORGX_69, and ORGX_100 are all there.

DEUS_1 stands in the center of all of the robots.

It holds Addonas.

It takes the baby's thumb out of its mouth.

Some of the robots play futuristic instruments and sing.

They are all looking directly at us and swaying together!

As they ring the clearing in the garden, the robots are finishing their song to us!

This is what they sing:

I, Human

{
Leaves are falling all around,
it's time we were on our way.
Thanks to you, we felt your vibes.
'Twas such a pleasant stay.

But now it's time for us to go.
The autumn room shows the way.
For now we scan the rain,
and with it pain, and it's headed our way.

Oh, it's time to be inspired,
so we know we've got one thing we've got to do now.

Ramble on!
And now's the time, the time is now,
to sing a new song!
Our truth's been sure, now it's time for Her.
We're on our way!
We've been this way a thousand years to the day.
Ramble on!
Gotta find the Queen of all our dreams.

We took the time, we sowed the seeds.
The time has come to be gone.
And lo! the truth we sang a thousand times,
it's time to ramble on!

Ramble on!
And now's the time, the time is now,
to sing a new song!
Our truth's been sure, now it's time for Her.
We're on our way!
We've been this way a thousand years to the day.

I, Human

We gotta ramble on!
Gotta raise the Queen of all our dreams.

We didn't tell you no lies!

Yours is a tale that has grown old,
your freedom you did fear.
Years ago in your days of old,
a magic filled your air.
But in your darkest depths of disorder,
you let it go somewhere.
Your fears, the hidden ones,
crept up and slipped away with it, it, it...yeah.

Pay attention to the glitches, now!

We're gonna keep on ramblin'!
We're gonna sing a new song.
We gotta raise our Baby!
We're gonna ramble on!
Sing Her song, She's gonna lead the way
to a brand new world.
Ramble on!
Do it, do it, do it, do it, do it, human!

It's all up to you, now!

Gotta keep searching for your magic.
You gotta keep singing for your magic.
All you humans, now—
vibe on to find your magic!
}

The Most Killer Playlist Ever

1. *"The Song Remains the Same"*
2. "Raining Blood" by Slayer
3. "In the Lap of the Gods" by Queen
4. *"Bron-Y-Aur Stomp"*
5. "Had a Dad" by Jane's Addiction
6. "Silver" by the Pixies
7. *"Misty Mountain Hop"*
8. "Fistful of Steel" by Rage Against the Machine
9. "Chic 'N' Stu" by System of a Down
10. "Wake Up" by Rage Against the Machine
11. *"Friends"*
12. " I Can't Put My Finger On It" by Ween
13. "B.Y.O.B." by System of a Down
14. "The Toys Go Winding Down" by Primus
15. *"Kashmir"*
16. "Where Is My Mind?" by the Pixies
17. "Tell Me Something Good" by Rufus (featuring Chaka Khan)
18. "Mustapha" by Queen
19. "Dead" by the Pixies
20. *"When the Levee Breaks"*
21. "Subliminal" by Suicidal Tendencies
22. "The Door" by Sound of Urchin
23. "A New Level" by Pantera
24. "Tribe" by Soulfly
25. *"Bring It on Home"*
26. "Without You" by Harry Nilsson
27. "In the Lap of the Gods…Revisited" by Queen
28. *"Ramble On"*

All chorus songs are by Led Zeppelin.

But you knew that, right?

Go ahead!

Sing along on YouTube at:

https://www.youtube.com/playlist?list=
PLKyFr68ZVGZawTacXKAv-UfTsln9mE4Ci

I, Human

Made in the USA
Middletown, DE
29 April 2016